Broken Arrow
Press

Praise for D. László Conhaim's
Comanche Captive

"Fast-paced … unusual … With *Comanche Captive*, D. László Conhaim makes the unusual choice of telling the story of a woman's resolute quest after she is taken from the band of Indians who had captured her. With drama, humor, and vivid detail, he creates an unflinching view of the harsh complexities of life on the frontier."

— Lucia St. Clair Robson,
bestselling author of *Ride the Wind*

"A deftly crafted and simply riveting read from cover to cover … very highly recommended."

— *Midwest Book Review*

"Conhaim offsets this brutal tale of human cruelty, injustice, and violence with rich descriptions of the natural beauty of the West. Recommended."

— *Library Journal*

"*Comanche Captive*'s rich characterizations bring a fascinating period of American history to life … page turning … thought provoking."

— Michael Belfiore,
author of *The Department of Mad Scientists*

"A great historical novel."

— WISR, Pennsylvania

Praise for
All Man's Land

"Conhaim draws on various elements of the classic Western ... to tell a story inspired by his longtime fascination with the singer and activist Paul Robeson ... Benjamin is a compelling, multilayered protagonist who moves beyond his Robeson inspiration ... The prose is vivid and often dramatic, which makes for a memorable read ... A well-developed and thoughtful novel of right and wrong in the Old West."

—*Kirkus Reviews*

"Inspired by the music and life of Paul Robeson, D. László Conhaim's *All Man's Land* ... reminds the reader that the most unlikely of relationships can form even in spaces where they should not exist ... Seeing the humanity in another person is a meaningful sub-theme ... We are battling, still, with many of the themes addressed in this book ... I thoroughly enjoyed [it] ... It is a book that should be read in classrooms and community book clubs. It is one to add to the discussion of race relations as this country should be *All Man's Land*."

—Christian Starr,
ThyBlackMan.com

"A fictional tribute to renaissance man Paul Robeson, *All Man's Land* is a solid literary work ... of social inspection, historical precedent, and cultural insights ... As Benjamin Neill wields the Jewish Kaddish and guns alike, readers will delight in a story that is far more literary and intellectual than the typical Western entertainment. *All Man's Land* weaves a powerful story of how times change, and how one man's purpose becomes an inspiring message for new generations."

—*Midwest Book Review*

"The exploration of a black-Jewish relationship in frontier times would seem challenge enough, but Conhaim blends this reality-based novel with a striking consideration of the overall prejudices and sentiments of the times, injecting fictional drama and embellishments into a kind of memoir that is absorbing and enlightening on many levels ... As Conhaim paints a portrait of David, a young man who prompts Benjamin Neill to examine his own prejudices and purposes, readers receive a solid blend of frontier conflict and the evolution of challenging relationships ... *All Man's Land* returns to a world that has largely moved away from Western popular fiction and memories of Paul Robeson, but it lives on as a tribute to this powerful individual and resurrects a sense of his multifaceted talents while providing a social commentary on America's early years."

—*Donovan's Bookshelf*

ALL MAN'S LAND

Defiance wasn't enough

D. László Conhaim

ALL MAN'S LAND

Paperback Edition

Broken Arrow Press, 2566 West Lake of the Isles Pkwy, Minneapolis, MN 55405, USA

brokenarrow908@gmail.com

Cover design by Avital David at upwork.com
Interior design by Velin@Perseus-Design.com
Logo by Michael R. Geffen
Author photo by Boaz Rabinovitch

First edition published June 2019

ISBN 978-0-9843175-1-6

Visit the author's website: dlaszloconhaim.com

For my daughter, Shir, my son, Ziv,
and for my wife, Inbal

Contents

Introduction

The story and the man
behind *All Man's Land*

While exploring my grandparents' record collection in the cellar of my family home in 1986, age 17, I made a life-altering discovery. In my hands was an album cover graced with the statesmanlike visage of an African-American man, the name *Robeson* emblazoned below his chin. Judging by the artist's seasoned appearance, this was obviously no introductory album, but a breakout of another sort.

In my possession, I would learn, was the prized 1958 Vanguard LP marking the return of Paul Robeson to the international arena after almost a decade of enforced confinement in the United States, where his great voice had been all but silenced.

Before long I was listening, captivated, to the haunting first track, "Water Boy," on which Robeson in his magnificent bass baritone wails a plea for refreshment while busting rocks on a chain gang. This was more than a voice, and more than a listening experience. The scholar Robert O'Meally has said that Robeson sings with "the might and authority of God."

To hear what he means, just treat yourself to a Robeson recording of "Go Down Moses."

Paul Robeson is a presence to be absorbed, to be reckoned with, his spirit full of fight, his music his sword. On that 1958 Vanguard recording, backed by a powerful chorus, his songs of hardship are imbued with a survivor's heroism, a bruised champion's vindication—for, after a taxing struggle of his own against the state, he was free again to record, to travel, and to perform and speak his mind to adoring audiences around the world.

That night over dinner, I innocently asked my parents, "Who was Paul Robeson?"

Stunned, they reacted in unison. "*Who* was Paul Robeson!"

Call and response.

I began work on *All Man's Land* two years later. At the time, I was spending a summer abroad in Tokyo, where I'd rented a room on the second floor of a Buddhist temple called Shinshin-en. Initially the story was simply about a mysterious stranger, who, while seeking revenge in a frontier town for untold reasons, forms a bond with a young man. Sound familiar? One day I awoke to the story's unoriginality—part *Shane*, part *The Man from Laramie*, two favorite 1950s Hollywood westerns. Either I could abandon the project or do something different with it. I fretted at my desk. Then, while loading a Robeson cassette tape—possibly to drown out the monks' chanting in the sanctuary below—I got the idea to make the hero black. Next, I made the boy Jewish. The story gradually metamorphosed as the music drove, influenced, and informed the work. The more my story fell under Robeson's spell, the more prominent became the black-Jewish acquaintanceship at its heart.

* * *

In 1991 or '92, the editor who discovered Robert Ludlum recommended an early draft of *All Man's Land* to the editorial board at Crown where it "failed to receive company-wide support." Unable to get subsequent traction with it, I eventually moved on to other projects, co-founding *The Prague Revue* in 1995 through which I published a second novel, *Autumn Serenade*, in the Czech Republic in 1999.

* * *

Volumes have been written on Paul Robeson. Of them I especially recommend *Paul Robeson* by Martin Duberman and *Paul Robeson Speaks* edited by Philip S. Foner. In the latter digest, the annotated chronology of his accomplishments from 1917 is awe-inspiring: All-American football star and Rutgers valedictorian, Columbia Law School graduate, lawyer, singer, actor of stage and screen, and global champion of racial and social justice. A tenacious autodidact, he also trained himself in linguistics and musicology and commonly featured in his concert appearances a segment demonstrating similarities in melodies from around the world.

I also recommend Robeson's 1958 autobiography and self-defense, *Here I Stand*. Why a self-defense?

In 1949, Robeson had brought disaster upon himself by making reckless statements in Paris and Stockholm which questioned whether black Americans would fight for a country that oppressed them against one in which they lived in "full human dignity" (the U.S.S.R.).* A firestorm at home erupted, and it didn't help matters when the Soviets—as if poking America in the eye—then named a mountain after him. In

---

* See pp. 135-136 for disagreement over Robeson's Paris statement.

1950, the U.S. State Department revoked his passport and, consequentially, extinguished the international performing career of one of America's most famous artists. Robeson's resulting confinement from 1950-58 constituted an outrageous abuse of legislative and judicial power, legal only under an antidemocratic Act of Congress.

But let's return to his music in closing. My favorite release is the posthumous *Odyssey of Paul Robeson*, a collection of homemade recordings from his confinement years when record labels would not record him, radio stations would not play his music, and electronic media outlets would not air his views.

The stirring, introspective qualities of the studio recordings in Parts I and III convey a moving counterpoint to the vexing legal battles he was waging concurrently against the state. Robeson, singing in a relaxed and intimate manner— as if to himself—reminds me of Cicero, forcibly retired from politics by Caesar and instead occupied at home with the composition of his sublime philosophical treatises.

Similarly muted and perhaps equally affected by hubris, Paul Robeson made his best music in solitude.

DLC
Tel Aviv,
May 2019

"For he is a lover of his country who rebukes and does not excuse its sins."

— Frederick Douglass

Chapter One

A lone rider dismounted outside the Sun and Sagebrush Inn and stepped out of the driving rain. Sheltered by the porch overhang, he rested his rifle on the shoulder of his slicker and gave final glances up and down Main Street, where armed men stood guard in the deluge. There was no turning back. Before him the doors could swing toward a hospitable reception or open into a torrent of lead. He breathed in and pushed through, ready to lower his rifle and fire.

Inside to his right a group of men were gathered at the bar, some standing, others seated on a few stools. Some had just backed away from the windows. His gaze flitted from hip to hip. He saw belts but no slings and holsters. A sign above the cash register read *Check Guns With Bartender*. Reassured, he removed his wide-brimmed hat, spilling a sheet of rainwater on the floor.

The proprietress wasn't amused. "Want a drink? Or a mop?"

Startled by the sound of a woman's voice, he watched her appear from behind the line of men. Voluptuous and, it appeared, corset-less, Sally Murphy was perhaps forty years old.

"My apologies," he said, running a hand through his wiry graying hair. "I seem to have left my manners on the porch."

"That's typical over at the *Saloon*," she replied. "How about that drink?"

"Whiskey," he answered, scanning the dining area over his left shoulder—a few empty tables and a sagging piano.

"Then disarm, mister."

After a moment's hesitation, he laid his Winchester on the counter and pushed it across to Sally. When she offered the faintest of smiles in return, he pulled off his gloves and parted the sides of his slicker to reveal two Colt .44 caliber revolvers. More than a single observer flinched at the sight of his tied-down double six-guns sheathed in historic Union-issued carbine boots.

Careful to avoid sparking a reaction from somebody with a hidden weapon, the rider left his sidearms in their encasements. He unfastened his hip sling and handed the whole thing over to Sally before leaning into the bar.

She received it with some curiosity, stowing it below.

Stuck to the mirror opposite him was a certificate illustrated with the profile of Abraham Lincoln and a banner reading *Lincoln Legion*. He squinted to make out the message:

I HEREBY ENROLL IN THE LINCOLN LEGION AND PROMISE, WITH GOD'S HELP, TO KEEP THE FOLLOWING PLEDGE, WRITTEN, SIGNED AND ADVOCATED BY ABRAHAM LINCOLN: WHEREAS, THE USE OF INTOXICATING LIQUORS AS A BEVERAGE IS PRODUCTIVE TO PAUPERISM, DEGRADATION AND CRIME; AND BELIEVING IT IS OUR

DUTY TO DISCOURAGE THAT WHICH PRODUCES MORE
EVIL THAN GOOD, WE THEREFORE PLEDGE OURSELVES
TO ABSTAIN FROM THE USE OF INTOXICATING LIQUORS
AS A BEVERAGE.

The rider might have chuckled but his attention was suddenly drawn to the faces of curious youngsters appearing at the windows to his right—four, five, now six boys fogging the glass with their anxious breath.

He untied his neckerchief and stuffed it damp into a coat pocket. "Been stormy in these parts long?" he asked Sally.

She opened her mouth to reply but one of her customers answered for her:

"Thunderheads rolled in ahead of you." The wisp of a man slipped in next to him on his left side, clutching a whiskey glass. His breath reeked of drink and gum disease.

"Don't you listen to him, mister," said Sally. "Been cloudy all week."

"Maybe they'll blow out with you too." The scrawny man was undeterred.

With an air of disappointment the rider merely stared downward into the cowpoke's jittery eyes.

"You why Marshal Neill left town this morning? Word's been a-spreadin'."

The rider threw back his whiskey. "Gone is he?"

In the dimness of the bar the haggard cowboy's teeth appeared as dark as Kentucky bourbon. He stepped up against the rider with a menace that could've frightened a jackrabbit.

"If you means to linger hereabouts the marshal might just find you perforated."

"Step back, Carvey," Sally snapped, "or get off my property. What're you fixing to do—breathe him to death?"

Jack Carvey thrust his glass forward. "How about another little drinkie, Sally?"

After giving him a hard look, Sally splashed his glass.

Carvey gulped it down and wiped his chin with the back of his hand. "I don't pay for short pours," he said, then burst into a boozy cackle and swaggered—with a misstep or two—to the doors.

The rider turned on his heel, gracefully for a big man.

"My gun, Sally," Carvey demanded before transferring his unsteady gaze back to the rider.

Sally's worried look also shifted to the dark newcomer at the bar. The stranger nodded while sneaking a hand behind his lapel. With a sigh she placed a six-gun on the counter and slid it down to Carvey.

Holstering it clumsily, he spit at the floor and shot her a contemptuous eye. "Done drunk my last in this stinkin' hole."

"Ever ponder why it stinks when you pay a call?" she retorted. "I'll send the marshal over with your tab."

The sound of flapping doors signaled Carvey's stumbling departure. But first he had scowled at the rider and called him a nigger.

* * *

Sally wiped her brow with her sleeve.

"I wish to secure lodgings for a day or two," said the rider after a restorative pause. "Be so kind as to show me to a room."

"Think that's a good idea?"

"Unless you'd recommend another place...."

"Not if you want to see tomorrow."

"Then I should accept your hospitality."

"I reckon you got a right to it," she said for the others to hear. "My helper will stable your horse and deliver your bags."

"What about my weapons?"

"They stay with me till you exit the premises."

"Then I hope you're a good shot."

She motioned for him to follow her. He admired her curves as she gracefully ascended the stairs. "I'll put you in the corner room, number Nine. Unless you prefer one in the middle."

"I'll take the corner one," he replied. "Which rooms are occupied?"

"Just number Three—by another traveler." Sally opened the door and flipped a switch, illuminating a brass chandelier above the bed. He stepped inside. The sole window faced east. Wind and rain lashed the glass.

When he turned around at the sound of her dangling the key chain his tremendous shadow enshrouded her and she stepped back. "You'll find the bathroom next to the stairs. We got plenty of water by pump and pipe from Lodgepole Creek. Even an electric boiler."

"A hot bath sounds mighty fine." He hadn't shaved or bathed since riding out of Denver. Until an hour ago he was caked with dust; now he was sodden with mud.

"I'll draw the water. Towels will be waiting for you. Four bits a bath. Meals thirty-five cents and up. Beds two dollars a night. I'll total all expenses, including your bar tab, at the end of your stay."

"That's optimistic," he said.

"For your sake and mine do your drinking here. Avoid Klyde's Saloon."

"*Klyde's.* Would that establishment happen to belong to somebody named O'Brien?"

"Why, yes, Klyde O'Brien." Her eyes narrowed. "Know him?"

"Could be."

She stepped away and changed the subject. "As you can probably guess from Carvey's welcoming cheer, our town ain't a popular watering hole with colored travelers. I regret how you were treated."

"Forget it. That mosquito didn't draw blood. And I didn't swat him."

"We don't have many mosquitoes out here. But we got plenty of bloodsuckers," she said. "Mister, I'm glad to have you as a guest. Sally's my name."

"I'm called Benjamin Neill."

"Neill? Ain't that a coincidence. Our marshal's name is Neill."

"So it is," he said. "Will I see you at breakfast?"

"I'll be riding shotgun for you."

"I thank you, Sally."

Benjamin shut the door and got out of his slicker. Strapped to his plaid shirt was a pregnant shoulder holster. Unfastening it, he took another look around the room.

Below the bed lay a finely woven serape whose dominant reds matched those of the coverlet. Next to the bed were a night table and lamp. A stone fireplace slumbered in the opposite wall. Against the far wall was a small desk and above it hung an uninspired oil painting of a mounted rider in silhouette crossing a sun-washed prairie. Benjamin Neill wasn't moved by the scene until he read the title tagged on its frame: *All Man's Land.*

22

He draped the shoulder holster over a chair next to the door and switched off the chandelier. Then he moved to the window and peered out. Tumultuous clouds were fading into darkness. Bending to untie the curtain knots he winced from the familiar aches of a long journey. He seated himself on the bed and as he was straining to pull off his boots a knock came at the door.

"Your bag, mister?"

The door creaked open and a young man tottered inside, grappling with Benjamin's saddlebags slung over one arm and a noose bag slung over his shoulder. With effort he lowered the sack to the floor. Next, he draped the saddlebags beside the conspicuous holster hanging from the chair. He was of average height and build, dark-haired, around twenty years old.

He indicated the cinched sack as he caught his breath.

"What's in that one—rocks?"

"No, books."

"Books?"

Benjamin rose to tower over the boy. He found a dime in his pocket and laid it in his hand.

"Thanks, mister! Miss Murphy says while you're in the tub she'll light you a fire. Darn nippy tonight…."

"What do they call you, young man?"

"David."

"A beautiful name."

"Seems to fit me all right."

Benjamin smiled. "Ever read the Bible?"

"Yeah, I know—David … and Goliath." He returned the smile. Nervously, he gestured down to the bag of books. "You a preacher?"

"No. But I teach."

"You a teacher, then?"

"No. But at times I have striven to guide."

David backed into the light of the corridor. "I'll brush down your horse tonight. If you need him tomorrow, just stop by the stables in back. I'm usually in earshot."

"All right. I'll give you a holler."

"Mister," said David, pointing at the scabbard slung over the chair, "what're all the firearms for?"

Benjamin put his hands on his hips. "For protection. And sometimes instruction."

"You come to instruct our marshal?"

"Maybe."

"He ain't here, gone to Cheyenne. Sure left town in a hurry. Ain't like him to avoid somebody. How'd he know you was coming?"

"That's a good question."

"Won't be back for days."

"I can wait."

"For what?" asked David.

"You're an inquisitive one, aren't you?"

"Everybody in town's wondering what you're fixing to do."

"Aren't you afraid I might shoot you for asking?"

"A little," said David. "But I reckon you won't."

Benjamin nodded, exasperated. "I'll get some rest now, David."

* * *

After closing time at his saloon, Klyde O'Brien sat playing poker with four of his men. A cloud of cigar smoke lingered about the massive brass chandelier that hung overhead like a giant spider. Jack Carvey, never reluctant to pull a cork, was presently slurring a question to his boss:

"Why'd the marshal order us to keep a distance from that old nigger?"

The monstrous O'Brien relit his cigar and leaned back in his chair—causing its joints to complain—and studied his lackeys' critical faces one by one. He expelled a plume of smoke and rolled the cigar between his stubby fingers. "I reckon he'll explain why when he returns from Cheyenne."

Slim Barker, another of O'Brien's closest cowpokes, spoke next. "There's talk goin' round about that Negro knowin' Marshal Neill from times past. Ain't you been acquainted with Neill since you was boys?"

O'Brien became irritable whenever anybody alluded to his past with Marshal Neill. Their friendship indeed predated their settling in Wyoming territory, its roots in the antebellum South. About those early years the townspeople knew only that O'Brien had worked on the Neill family plantation until it was burned to ashes by the Army of the Potomac. Marshal Neill had O'Brien's word he would never reveal more.

"Don't you boys fret over it," said O'Brien, conscious of his unconvincing tone.

Old Jesse Larcan bent forward. "Klyde, that man is armed every which way."

"There's no law in these parts says a Negro can't bear arms." O'Brien picked up his cards again in an attempt to renew interest in the game. "I ain't concerned."

Carvey turned his foul breath on the lean, clean-shaven Kev Holt, sitting next to him. "I reckon we needn't be with Kev among us. Concerned, that is."

Holt had been passing through town two days before when, after demonstrating his marksmanship, O'Brien tapped him as a useful—if probably impermanent—addition to his clan. Holt grimaced. "Mind not leaning in so close?"

O'Brien, Barker, and Larcan all convulsed in laughter while Carvey crimsoned. Klyde cleared his throat. "Jack's got a point, Kev. Think you could take him? I mean, you showed me your expertise shooting spokes and bottles, but…."

Holt cocked an eyebrow. "I saw him from a long remove this afternoon. But he seemed mortal to me." He picked up his cards.

"Mortal?" asked Carvey. "We supposed to know what that means?"

O'Brien lost his temper. "If you ain't aware of mortality, Jack, why didn't you try putting a bullet in his brain?"

"But I thought we wasn't supposed to—"

"Oh, bite it off, Jack."

Jesse Larcan almost choked laughing. Then, "What would we do without your fast draw, Kev?"

"Get yourselves shot?"

"Let's not make any assumptions, Mr. Holt," said O'Brien. "We'll just sit tight till Marshal Neill gets back."

Chapter Two

Next morning the bustling breakfast crowd at the Sun and Sagebrush Inn fell silent when Benjamin lumbered down the stairs, an imposing sight in his sweeping slicker and broad hat. His quick appraisal of the dining hall registered not a single empty seat. Sally immediately came around from behind the bar and hurried over to him. The din of conversation gradually picked up as they exchanged greetings at the foot of the stairs.

"Twice the usual number of customers," she whispered, "and they've kept ordering refills—waiting, I presume, for you to make your entrance. I had to save you a chair and open an extra tin of coffee beans." At once she dragged the chair out from behind the bar.

The nearest table was occupied by a matronly group.

"Make way, ladies, for an extra place setting!"

Giddy affirmations broke their hush.

Sally pushed her new boarder into his seat and took his order. When she left them alone, Benjamin affably addressed his company in a honeyed voice, "So what's the big news around town these days?"

The ladies giggled.

"You are," said one, batting her eyes.

"Really? How come?"

The ladies glanced bashfully at one another. "Well, you certainly are big!"

After more titters, Benjamin responded, "Six feet three inches and shrinking."

They laughed.

"And you certainly are black," one exclaimed.

"Oh, Mildred, really!" another protested.

"Black as the coffee I drink, but sweetened with sugar."

"Brown sugar?" asked the first to speak.

More giggles and nudging ensued, and small talk, until Sally rejoined them with Benjamin's breakfast, a rush order. Before him, she served a dish whose contents were arranged into a smiley face: eggs for eyes, biscuit for the nose, and slices of bacon for upturned lips.

Benjamin angled the plate toward his companions. "Why, it's me...."

"That's what we call a custom breakfast," said Sally, pouring his mug full. "No cream," she added with a wink.

Just then, the inn's other boarder, a prickly and rotund traveler named Ficklewright, came tumbling down the stairs with his suitcase and went straight for the back door, presumably headed to the stables for his hitch and horse.

"Planning on squaring your bill?" Sally called after him. "I got it behind the bar!"

Ficklewright answered by wheeling around and pointing a fat finger at Benjamin. "You don't mean I'm expected to pay!" Resuming his flight, he threw open the door and squeezed through with his bag.

Benjamin rose from his seat but Sally was first out the door behind Ficklewright, and before Benjamin could make it outside the altercation had already begun—the thudding of luggage into the mud; a cry of "bitch"; a slap. He reached the scene in time to witness Sally deliver a second blow. Ficklewright toppled backward into the muck.

Young David came running out of the stables.

The mud-spattered, blinking Ficklewright retrieved a handkerchief from his rear pocket. He attempted to nurse a bloody nose but merely smeared mud on his face. Then he began to cry.

"Your whimpering won't help." Sally regarded David. "Throw his saddle in the manure pile."

"Yes, ma'am!"

"Mush it in real good."

"Sure will!"

"Aw, hell," Ficklewright squealed, peeling himself from the ground. "I'll pay up, I'll pay up!"

Before Sally showed him her backside she told David to collect his money and rig his horse.

Ficklewright rolled himself to his knees, popping his vest buttons one by one.

"You're doomed, lady," he shouted after her. But his words stopped at the door Sally slammed behind herself and Benjamin.

* * *

Breakfast concluded, Benjamin left through that same door shortly thereafter, buckling his hip sling as he crossed to the stables. He found the gate open. Inside to the right was David, sitting at a desk in the tack room and poring over a thick book. Sensing a presence behind him, the boy swung around to see Benjamin silhouetted in the doorway.

"Damn! You gave me a scare."

"I only hesitated because you seemed absorbed in your reading."

"Short break from my chores," he replied with a trace of shyness. "Want to take your horse out?"

"Sure do!"

David rose, glancing demurely toward the desk. "Wait here, mister." He went off through the narrow interval dividing the stalls.

Benjamin appraised the orderly stables, noticing that all the implements and effects were in their proper places. The air was sweetly fragrant of hay. Displayed on the walls were the requisite horseshoes and photographs, along with a pair of postcards. One, entitled *Going Places*, showed a cowboy being bucked from the saddle of a superimposed rabbit. Curious, Benjamin pulled the tack pinning the card and flipped the picture over. On the obverse side was a one-cent stamp of Benjamin Franklin and a postmark from Denver Station. A personal note read:

> *Dear David,*
> *Thought you'd like this one, too.*
> *Visit with Cousin Albert nice.*
> *He's the same, only much older.*
> *Be home soon.*
> *Love,*
> *Jeannie*

Benjamin reaffixed the postcard and focused on the other. Entitled *Barbering in the Cow Camp*, the colored photograph merely showed some cowboys getting haircuts and shaves. No magic in this picture. Moving on, Benjamin trained his attention on a framed tintype of what appeared to be a town council assembled on the porch of the Sun and Sagebrush Inn. In the rear stood Sally, and next to her a thinly mustached and stone-faced man with unruly grey hair— James Neill. Benjamin tapped the glass over his visage before turning his gaze toward David's desk. In contrast to the tidy surroundings, the desk was cluttered with personal items: a mirror, a hairbrush, a photograph of a husband and wife in a shiny brass frame, an open sketchpad filled with drawings of horses, and finally a tattered copy of the Old Testament.

"I'm right confounded," said David while leading the towering stallion, some sixteen hands high, toward the gate. "Square fifteen-by-twenty-inch skirts, wooden ox bow stirrups, latigo cinches, and double-rigged for one-man stock roping. Judging from your equipment I'd say you do your share of cowpunching. But then, there's your blue saddle blanket and this—" David handed the canteen to Benjamin "—I've seen this type at Frontier Day in Cheyenne. The cavalry at Fort Russell and Fort Sanders use 'em. I just can't figure you out, mister."

"You needn't bother," replied Benjamin, eyes still searching. "Do you occupy a room here?"

The boy pointed to the loft. "Up-ladder. Somebody's gotta look after our guests' property."

"Good to know it." Benjamin clipped the canteen to his saddle. "And if you don't mind my asking ... whereabouts does your family reside?"

David wiped his brow and pointed at the framed picture on the desk. "Them was my folks. My mother died in childbirth. My father passed away last year."

"My deepest sympathies. Any brothers or sisters?"

He shook his head.

"How'd you come to work for Sally and make this your sole residence?"

"My father had been borrowing from the bank so I was forced to forfeit the house to Klyde O'Brien to fix the accounts."

"I'm beginning to understand," said Benjamin.

After a pause, David indicated the horse. "Where you going to take him, mister?"

Benjamin slid a worn boot into the stirrup, clapped a hand over the mane, and climbed onto his mount. Crowned with the big hat, he answered, "Oh ... around."

"That what the weapons are for?"

"Maybe."

"Most of the land north of here belongs to Klyde O'Brien," said David. "I'd head south if I was you."

"If I *were* you."

"We don't talk eastern talk out here—but I notice you do."

Benjamin tipped his hat. As he reined his horse into the damp morning air he called to David over his shoulder. "Come by my room tonight for a closer look-see at those books!"

David hastily assented with thanks, his words trailing after clumps of dirt the animal kicked up as it trotted away. When he returned to his reading he found a pencil stub inserted into the text, marking the story of David and Goliath.

* * *

Benjamin guided his horse into a less than crowded Main Street and glanced around at the townspeople who promptly abandoned their comings and goings to gawk. He tried nodding at some. For the most part his greetings were rewarded with cold stares but a few men tipped their hats and several women managed polite smiles. Could be worse, he thought. He let his gaze wander over the shop signs: *Mercantile—"Lowest Prices, Highest Quality," Nathan's Carriage House, Flynn's Clothiers, Wells Fargo Bank, Bjorgen Drug, U.S. Post Office, Dry Cleaning and Laundry, High Plains Harness and Saddlery, Locksmith, Confectionery, Brown Produce, McLean Window Shop, O'Brien Real Estate,* and further ahead on the right, *Klyde's Saloon.*

Inside the Saloon, Beatrice O'Brien, Klyde's plump wife, burst into the stockroom where her husband was making notes on a clipboard. "Klyde! He's heading straight for the Saloon!"

O'Brien raised his alarmed eyes. "On foot or mount?"

Hearing he was mounted, Klyde threw down his clipboard and hastened to the bar, behind which he hauled out his Sharps buffalo rifle. He cocked it and headed for the door.

Benjamin stopped his horse before the blood-red facade of Klyde's Saloon. A bog of mud and manure lay below the knobby hitching rails. Stained-glass windows framed the double-door entrance. Behind the window to his right, Benjamin could make out the shadowy, diffuse form of somebody peering out. Suddenly the figure jerked left toward the batwing doors.

The doors parted to reveal Klyde O'Brien brandishing his rifle. Benjamin let fall the reins and dropped his hands near the walnut grips of his guns. For what seemed like minutes the two men shared threatening glares.

At last Benjamin reined his stallion away. When he was a safe remove up Main Street, the townspeople, whose attention had followed his movements, focused instead on O'Brien, who now came out of his trance, glance flitting about the crowd.

* * *

Klyde O'Brien's endless holdings disappeared into the gloomy northern horizon: to the northeast, expansive pens held claret and white Herefords; to the northwest, the prairie was left open for his longhorns to wander. A mere fraction of O'Brien's total stock, this herd numbered no less than five thousand head—and unseasonably stormy weather threatened its survival. The normally lush grama grass had been alternately bombarded by hail and soaked by rain, then frozen by nightfall. The result was a blackened prairie all but absent of grazing material.

Benjamin ignored the signs warning trespassers and before long the anticipated drum of hoofbeats broke the calm. He reined his stallion eastward toward three men approaching on horseback, spotting Jack Carvey among them. As the men rode up, Benjamin unhurriedly removed his gloves. Jack Carvey, Slim Barker, and Kev Holt halted their quarter horses just spitting distance from him. Holt's roan was the only mount not rigged for wrangling.

The horses snorted and grunted in the cold.

"Can'tcha people read?" began Carvey. "Them signs yonder read no trespassin'!"

"They aren't legal," came the reply.

Slim Barker expectorated a wad of chaw. "They's the law if posted!"

Benjamin remained impassive. Carvey continued: "Time you was reminded what happens to niggers that don't know their place. Step down off that horse, thick lips. A sturdy tree awaits."

"Yeah? Where?" There were no trees in sight.

"I'm gonna drag you to one!"

The silent figure of Kev Holt was last to lower his hands.

In a low voice, Benjamin told Carvey, "If it's a lynching you want, you'll be first. That's a promise from these thick lips."

Carvey reassured the others with worldly authority: "Ain't met a blacky yet who was good to his word."

Benjamin arched his eyebrows. "Well, you must be the village idiot."

Holt threw an inquisitive look at Carvey. Then Carvey and Barker attempted to draw. Benjamin's shots rang out instantly, his aim directed at their horses' hooves.

The trio's mounts bolted in three directions.

As Carvey lurched past, Benjamin reached out with his free hand and clawed his face, ripping him from the saddle. Carvey landed back first in the sludge with a crash of spurs and a squirt of chaw. Dazed and dripping tobacco, he raised himself by the elbows to see Benjamin's revolver aimed between his eyes.

"Unbuckle your sling and throw it aside."

The color had vanished from Carvey's face. He searched for his friends.

"Do it!"

Carvey wrestled himself to his knees, eyes glassy and pleading. With a groan of capitulation he unfastened the gun belt and tossed it aside.

"Get on your feet! Good. Now turn around and fetch your mount."

Delaying, Carvey wiped his palms against his filthy chaps.

"Do as I tell you!"

Then came the rhythmic pounding of hooves tearing up the ground.

Carvey glanced hopefully over his shoulders. But before his consorts could get close there was a whipping of air around him, a strip of shadow fell across his face. Benjamin's looped reins cinched his neck. Meantime, Barker and Holt rode up wildly, guns drawn. Holt was pointing his barrel skyward, a gesture not lost on Benjamin.

"Release your weapons," Benjamin ordered. Gripping the reins with his left hand, he was squeezing the life from Carvey while holding the others off with the gun in his right. Foaming at the mouth, Carvey was doing a puppet-like death dance.

Barker looked to Holt for direction. His reserved partner offered none.

"I said, release 'em," Benjamin thundered.

Holt holstered his six-gun with a sigh. Barker scowled and followed suit. Together they unbuckled their slings and let them fall to the ground.

Benjamin gave a final tug—eliciting a fresh flood of tears from his purpled victim—before abruptly releasing his grip. Carvey fell gasping. Benjamin holstered his weapon and eased back into his saddle. Unable to come to his aid, Barker and Holt watched dumbly as their partner writhed in agony in a muddy heap.

"You may scrape him up," Benjamin told them, "but first tie all three belts to a lone saddle."

The two men dismounted. Barker gathered up the belts and passed them to Holt who, in turn, fastened them to his saddle one at a time. Without prompting, Holt then performed the expected action—he made his horse bolt with a startling cry and a firm slap.

Benjamin fired his gun to keep her running.

Chapter Three

The sky was clear over Cheyenne.

In Capitol Park, an oval commons ringed and crossed by hickory chip paths, children delighted in fun and games while their matronly guardians languidly chewed the fat under latticed arbors. In stark contrast to this scene, a hatted figure whose coarse lapel shone with a gold star strode across the center lawn to the steps of the state capitol and through its open bronze portals. A minute later, after glancing at his pocket watch, he rapped on a door labeled *204 Attorney General Sam Clark.*

"Come on in!" a voice called.

Marshal James Neill stepped into an immaculate office appointed with a wet bar, grandfather clock, and a couch and three upholstered chairs arranged around a long mahogany coffee table. Sunlight poured through a line of windows overlooking the park. He shut the door.

"Howdy, Jim!"

Beautifully dressed in the western fashion, Sam Clark came around from behind his desk and offered Neill a brisk, familiar handshake.

Marshal Neill inquired after Clark's wife, two sons, and daughter. He'd first met them at the inaugural Cheyenne Frontier Day back in '97—a large-scale rodeo featuring unusual attractions, such as German Uhlans, British lancers, Russian Cossacks and even a mock skirmish between the U.S. Cavalry and the Sioux and Cheyenne. Marshal Neill and Sam Clark would later sit together on the annual event's planning committee alongside other Wyoming officials, including the owner and editor of *The Cheyenne Daily Sun*, Colonel E.A. Slack.

Ever gracious, Clark thanked Marshal Neill for his inquiry. "My wife's got Ronald and his sister Amy out at the races in Pioneer Park this afternoon. We're about to send Joe off to university on the East Coast. We worry he'll forget all about us."

"He'll come back," said Neill, "and not only for mom 'n' pop." With a wave of his hand, he indicated the magnificent southwesterly view through the windows. Rising from the distant prairie was the limitless sawtoothed range of the Rocky Mountains.

Clark shared Neill's enthusiasm for a vista that never failed to entrance. "Sometimes I just kick up my boots and recline here awestruck. You can even spot Boney Hair Peak rising from the ridge like a split toothpick."

He thrust a finger over the marshal's shoulder. "See, there…."

Neill nodded accordingly. "A familiar sight. I got a few of them myself, sprouting from my ears."

Adjusting his focus, Clark observed him closely. "I see…. You need a wife to yank 'em is all."

Neill grinned and shook his head—and thus his hat too, reminding him to take it off.

"Up north these days you can't see much past the rim of your hat," he said, "and the nights are positively bone chilling. A whole week of rain, even hail. Just keeps coming."

"Hard on cattle, crops." Clark took Neill's Stetson and placed it on a rack by the door.

"Hard on grazing material."

"I hear you, Jim," Clark responded with Neill now facing him. "That's why I've asked the Indian and General Land Offices to prioritize your friend Klyde O'Brien's petition to drive his herd north. Trouble is, that's been Cheyenne land since '84."

Marshal Neill slicked back his unwieldy grey hair. "But Klyde lobbied for Medicine Bow in the first place—to give the Cheyenne a secure home."

Clark shook a naughty-boy finger at him. "Or to get them off the pasture he wanted to the south. Trust me, Jim—we aim to protect our state's biggest herd. But any shifting of the tribe today will be temporary, consensual, and at a small profit to themselves."

"Or at a large profit for a longer duration," replied Marshal Neill, "but that's Klyde's business." He ran his thumb and forefinger up and down his thin mustache. "I'm here about something else."

"Well, whatever concerns you concerns me, Jim. But first, how about a drink? There's a fine bar right there for you to partake of. Just acquired a few bottles import."

"Not today."

"No? Then you have yourself a seat and start skinning the hide off this one for me." Clark pulled a cigarette case from his breast pocket and offered Marshal Neill a smoke.

Neill declined. "There's some trouble brewing in town."

Clark lit a cigarette. "Trouble? Something you can't handle yourself? Hard to believe, Jim."

The marshal shifted his weight on the couch.

"I may need you to consult the Justice Department."

"Justice?" From his seat opposite Marshal Neill, Clark made no attempt to disguise his shock. That Neill was appealing for help from anybody but Klyde O'Brien would have surprised any official in Wyoming. Once, the trail of a team of coach bandits had led a division of cavalry from Fort Russell into Main Street where the troops found a scattering of corpses. Neill and O'Brien, their rifles still smoking, were groin-kicking each to confirm death.

Clark blew a clumsy curl of smoke. "What's happening up there that might involve the Department of Justice?"

"The arrival of a certain colored visitor."

Clark guffawed. "That all?"

"This morning at Dyer's Hotel, I got a cablegram from Klyde. Says this individual's got folks trembling down to their boots. Nearly expired one of his men yesterday. Jerked him up by the neck with his reins."

"So? Throw him in jail. Run him out of town!"

"Can't do that from down here, can I? Anyway, it seems he was acting in self-defense after some of Klyde's boys tried to rough him up. He strayed onto his land."

"Unavoidable given Klyde's vast holdings," said Clark. "By law, non-penned grazing land is traversable to the general public, it has to be. But I suspect your people haven't much exposure to colored folk, except the occasional unit of buffalo soldiers. Doubtless they're apprehensive about a Negro visitor and it sounds like he isn't just passing through. So what's the reason behind his visit? And why'd *you* take the next train to Cheyenne?"

"I left *before* he came. Somebody in Denver alerted me. Colonel Slack's nephew."

"Young Stuart? Isn't he an apprentice at the *Post?*"

"Yep. Last week a colored writer there—name of Dunbar— was visited by another Negro. One who wore two guns on his belt. Stuart just happened to get his ear stuck to the wall of the office next to Dunbar's and overheard Dunbar identifying my town on a map. Stuart then checked with the reception desk and got the visitor's name. After that he consulted the *Post's* library and matched him with…." Neill paused. "Sam, he's not just anybody. He's the one we used to read about in the papers, the spokesman for his people. The *agitator.*"

Neill thought he saw Sam Clark wince.

A silence followed.

Clark tapped his cigarette on a polished silver ashtray. Then, "Even if Stuart is right about this fella, what danger is there of him organizing some sort of demonstration? You haven't any Negroes in your town."

"There's plenty here in Cheyenne and lots more in Denver."

The attorney general flashed Neill an alarmed look and took a deep drag on his cigarette. He smoothed his trouser leg. Neill gazed fixedly at him. He could hear the resonant ticking from the grandfather clock.

Clark finally looked up. "You're quite right bringing this to my attention before taking matters into your own hands.

I recollect that his activities were once investigated by the Justice Department. That inquiry might've resulted in a prosecution and lasting court orders. First, we need to know what transpired between him and the federal government. There happens to be somebody on my staff who worked at Justice and could be familiar with the case. You acquainted with Russ Cooper?"

"Can't say I am."

"Born here but educated in the East. Got his law degree at Yale and was automatically appointed to Attorney General Knox's staff in the last administration. Family connections. Now he's my deputy and someday he'll have my job. I'll get him to wire Washington today. Let's meet again tomorrow morning, first thing. A warning—Cooper's the pompous sort that practically begs for a punch in the nose. But he's thorough to a fault. Hold your temper and we'll both learn a lot. I didn't invite him on my staff for nothing."

Returning to Dyer's Hotel, Marshal Neill stopped in front of the old Bireen Stables with a look of astonishment. Under the signature banner that read *The Ride That Makes The Journey Easy* stood a half-dozen gleaming horseless carriages.

Chapter Four

That evening Sally was sipping brandy alone at the bar of the Sun and Sagebrush Inn. For an hour she had waited for more customers. To her satisfaction none had shown. She treasured a solitary evening now and then. And yet.... The wind outside had quit its howling and, in his room above, Benjamin was quietly singing spirituals to himself in an untrained but uncommonly beautiful bass baritone. In the hush downstairs she could make out almost every lyric. Was this his intention? Each song told a compelling story, transmitting vivid pictures to her of a suffering people remarkably full of hope. Sally had never known any Negro folk, never had the chance to know any. Until today she hadn't given much thought to their former slavery, nor had she ever considered their enduring oppression.

She could hardly restrain her curiosity about her new boarder and wondered if he would welcome a visit from her. He probably preferred to be left alone with his spirituals and with his contemplation. Still, what excuse could she find for going upstairs to check on him, to test his willingness to accept a casual visitor? She had not yet collected his laundry.

As she approached his room on the creaky floorboards the singing ceased. The door was slightly ajar, a positive sign. She knocked before peeking inside. Bootless but otherwise fully clothed in dungarees and a shirt unbuttoned almost to the navel, he was reclining against a stack of pillows at the top of the bed. A pile of books was arranged next to him. The fireplace crackled with a robust blaze.

"I've come for your washing," she said.

He pointed toward the door and with some effort began to rise.

"Don't trouble yourself!" She reached for the stuffed noose bag.

He arranged himself at the side of the bed.

"I trust you're comfortable here," she said from the doorway.

"Yes, quite."

"I was listening to you sing. It made me think."

Smiling, he responded, "That is often why I sing."

"Were you singing to make *me* think?"

His expression settled. "I sang because I felt the spirit moving in my heart."

"You a God-fearing man?"

"The spirit I felt was the spirit of my people," he said.

With that, Sally dropped the sack, stepped inside, and shut the door.

"Who are you?—and what do you have to do with our marshal?" she demanded.

But he didn't reply. Instead he patted the bedspread, encouraged by her bold move to place herself behind a closed door with him. Just how far would her boldness take her?

She sat next to him and repeated her question. Benjamin smiled again in return, and, leaning back on the palms of his hands, he recited a verse that sounded neither biblical nor spiritual: *"At last I saw a man, whose name I did not know—but he seemed for to be, a man of great authority...."* With a grave expression, he added, "I should keep that to myself, Sally."

"Every additional night here increases your risk."

"For a man of my people it's always dangerous to cross the country alone, even in these times."

"Word's spreading about what happened this morning," she whispered urgently. "They'll kill you for it. And they'll serve no time. Their boss is above the law."

Benjamin said nothing.

Sally placed a hand on his. "Trouble's coming on a locomotive from Cheyenne."

Benjamin was ready to reply when his whole body constricted in pain. Beneath her touch the muscles in his hand tensed.

"You're unwell...."

"It will pass," he said under his breath.

She pressed his hand.

After a pause: "I'll cause you to lose business, Sally. I wish I could compensate you for your losses."

"Don't be silly," she replied. But the allusion to money sparked a question. "How *do* you get by?"

"I pick up work where I can," he said. "Wrangling mostly in these parts."

She didn't believe him, despite the riggings of his horse.

"Getting a little old for that, ain't you?"

"That's a painful fact," he confessed. "I also—"

A noise outside the door halted his explanation. From under his pillows he withdrew his concealed gun. She gave him a scolding look for failing to surrender it before.

Another creak split the silence.

"Slip off your shoes."

She followed his instructions.

"Now get behind the door. When you're ready, swing it open."

Sally tiptoed over.

Benjamin positioned himself behind the bed, aiming his revolver at the polished wood door whose panels reflected the dancing firelight. The two exchanged glances.

He nodded and she performed her task.

A startled David was standing outside the room with a fist raised to knock. Seeing Benjamin's gun drawn he toppled backward with a cry. Benjamin let his weapon drop heavily onto the bed.

Sally revealed herself, and, reproaching the boy for not identifying himself, helped him up. Turning toward Benjamin, she indicated the gun.

"How come you didn't draw when I approached?"

"The door was open and I recognized your step."

Sally frowned, indicating the gun. "Better keep it close," she whispered. Then she grabbed her shoes and the washing and left.

"You're next, David," Benjamin sighed.

* * *

"I heard your voices," David confessed. "I wasn't sure I should interrupt."

"Well … since you're not dead, have a seat."

David closed the door behind him and filled the upholstered chair.

Benjamin assumed his previous position on the bed, next to his books—and the gun. "I'd almost lost hope of your calling."

David blushed.

"A young lady?"

"How'd you guess?"

"The trace of lip rouge on your right cheek."

Benjamin pivoted his body to rest his huge feet on the mattress, easing himself back against the pillows. "Nice girl?"

"Nice looking too," said David, trying to rub away the mark.

"Been courting her long?"

David blushed again. "A while."

"Would you be preparing to ask for her hand?"

"I'm afraid not."

"No?"

The youth looked away.

Benjamin leaned forward on his elbow.

"Does your being Jewish have anything to do with it?" he asked.

David's uneasy silence and averted gaze only caused Benjamin to add a nudging, "Perhaps?"

The boy folded his arms and fixed Benjamin with his blue eyes. "How come you know so much about me?"

"Simple observation. Your mother was wearing a *chai* about her neck in that photograph."

David was stunned. Was Benjamin's recognition of the *chai* the reason behind his invitation to visit? His presumptuous line of questioning began to make sense.

"But how do you know about such things? You're *colored*."

"Why shouldn't I recognize it? Its message is universal— life, health, prosperity. Besides, I count a few Jews among my friends." Benjamin leaned back, crossing his arms over his shirt. "Would your father have condoned a marriage between you? It would end your Jewish bloodline."

David scratched an imaginary itch on his furled brow.

"My folks should've considered that before laying down roots here," he replied.

"And how do you think her parents would react to your proposing?"

"I don't wonder. They say I'm no good, that my father was no good."

"That your people are no good?"

David nodded glumly.

"What does she think?"

"She's used to hearing stories about my father … I don't rightly know."

"Stories or lies?"

David considered whether or not to explain. What harm could it do? "When my folks first settled here the town was little more than Main Street, just a service and lodgings stop for frontier travelers. Back East my father had been a clothier. He figured that with the Saloon under construction and Cheyenne and Fort Russell nearby this place would boom someday. Spent his savings on the shop and brung in the latest fashions on the Transcontinental."

"How were you raised?—as a Jew?"

"My folks didn't follow the faith, as a couple that is."

"*Christianity* is a faith, Judaism more, but let's leave that for later. They concealed their heritage?"

"You could say that. But after my mother died, my father took to observing the Sabbath—partly for my sake, I reckon."

"And the truth got out."

The boy rubbed his nose with the back of his hand. "Maybe somebody peeped through the window one Friday night, or maybe somebody got to wondering why the shop was closed on Saturdays. Anyhow, when people realized we was … I mean, we *were* Jews my father lost favor fast. Neighbors who'd reached out to him after my mother's passing didn't take kindly to being deceived."

"Deceived? You mean your folks pretended otherwise?"

"They went to church," replied David.

Benjamin shook his head. "You needn't tell me more."

"Not common for somebody to show interest," the youth conceded.

"Then you won't mind if I ask your surname."

"It's Cohen."

"Cohen! With that name O'Brien and others might've suspected your folks were Jewish."

"Initially people heard the name as *Cohan,* so my parents adopted it. Went as far as to write their friends to address their mail accordingly. Still, they mostly kept to themselves."

"No wonder the girl's parents are suspicious of you. How'd the town react when people found out?"

"My father lost customers—and what friends he had. Then old man Flynn, who already owned several shops, started up his own clothier across the street. For lack of business, my father would sit by the window with a bottle of bourbon and stare out at Flynn's."

"Flynn of course did nothing to help your father."

To this David did not reply.

"A correct assumption?"

But David shook his head. "No, actually."

Few people had ever taken an interest in him before, certainly never a colored man. He hesitated.

"Don't feel obliged to respond out of courtesy," Benjamin added in a lighter tone.

David acknowledged that his new acquaintance was making predictable inquiries given his professed familiarity with Jews. As for himself, he had plenty of questions for Benjamin. The more he learned about him, the more he might discover about Marshal Neill. He looked up to Neill, yet suspected he was haunted by demons. Could Benjamin be one of them? Perhaps because it was the first time anybody other than Jeannie had broached the subject of his father's troubles he decided to reveal a secret he had long kept to himself.

"For years old man Flynn *helped* us. He wouldn't carry certain items, like some popular fabrics, so folks—mainly women—might patronize our place too. Some months he even helped us meet our obligations to O'Brien Real Estate."

"You owed money to O'Brien?" asked Benjamin. "Not to a bank?"

"There wasn't a bank for a long spell. The town sits on Mr. O'Brien's original claim, which he sold parcel by parcel. He acquired most of his holdings after a drought and cattle bust thirty years ago. Likely at O'Brien's urging, Flynn offered to buy us out."

"But of course he did." Benjamin raised his chin and his eyebrows settled low. "What'd your father say to that?"

"He considered it a sign the boom was close at hand. But first he had to avoid going bust. Then Flynn died, leaving his daughter the business. With Flynn gone my father was forced to borrow from the bank to satisfy his debt to Mr. O'Brien. That's when somebody started telling boldfaced lies about him. Word spread that because he was broke he was selling secondhand clothing at top dollar. That finished the shop, and my father's health went down with it. My folks come out here to start a new life. Instead it killed 'em both. Might kill me too."

"You could go back to your people," said Benjamin.

"Go back? I was born in this godforsaken place."

"And if your girl loves you, she might steal away with you, even go so far as to convert. It's happened before. Or are *you* the convert?"

David looked surprised. "One thing's for sure, I'm no city boy. Got no schooling except what I had at home. Got no experience, no money. And if Jeannie and I ran off, people'd come after us."

"You have the legal right."

"Has the law protected you?" Finally David could begin to satisfy his own curiosity. But he would need to wait a bit longer for answers to other questions.

"The law allows me to defend myself. So in a way it has protected me. But, I confess, it has been used against me too."

The fire crackled. From the street came a burst of drunken laughter. Then, in the quiet of the small room, Benjamin started humming, leading himself into a soft chant: "*When Israel was in Egypt's land—let my people go; oppressed so hard they could not stand—let my people go; Go down, Moses, way down in Egypt's land—tell ol' Pharaoh to let my people go."* His eyes ignited in the firelight. "Know it?"

"Can't say I do," replied David, his nervousness now spreading to his boots with one scratching the other. "Catchy though."

"It is *our* song of *your* people. And it has instilled courage in many a soul praying for deliverance."

"I ain't got much faith in God."

"That's less important than having faith in yourself." Benjamin sat up, his voice full of passion. "You obviously know little of your heritage. But I noticed you're reading the Old Testament and that's a good start. Your people's courageous self-respect, above all, has preserved your civilization—and that's what it is, a civilization, with faith at its core—down to today, while all those who oppressed the Israelites have disappeared. To cite the chant of a Jewish sage, *The Persians, what boast they?*—Our *ruler is above all rulers; the Romans, what boast they?*—Our *kingdom is above all kingdoms.* To realize your potential you must explore your identity, not hide it. Yet that is not enough. You must also open your eyes to other peoples, not look past them or turn away as most men do. And you should know something of the philosophies behind our fledgling and troubled democracy."

His unexpected sermon finished, Benjamin passed David his books one by one: Jean Jacques Rousseau's *The Social Contract*, David Walker's *Appeal to the Colored Peoples of America*, Frederick Douglass' *Narrative of the Life of Frederick Douglass*, and even Shakespeare's *Othello*. "Keep them," he said. "They're becoming burdensome to carry around."

"I'll read the books," replied David. "But for now, would you instruct me in a song or two? I can hold a tune, and your voice makes me want to sing along."

Benjamin gave David the broadest of smiles. "I'd be delighted. Here's one we can sing together…."

Chapter Five

Next morning Marshal James Neill and Russ Cooper exchanged greetings in Sam Clark's airy and bright Cheyenne office. Cooper was a pretty man in his late twenties wearing a tapered blue suit of European cut and cloth. At the wet bar the attorney general served them coffee from a shiny kettle. He gestured to the arrangement of furniture around his coffee table. The three men took their seats, Neill drawn to the familiar couch.

The marshal placed his porcelain cup on a matching saucer and cracked his knuckles. "I take it Washington responded."

While Clark lit a cigarette, Cooper, to his left at the end of the table, draped one leg over the other, revealing an embroidered boot. He reached into his breast pocket and withdrew a wad of cablegrams, setting them on the table between himself and Neill.

As if inviting the marshal to pick a card, he tapped the stack with a slender finger. "His life and times," he said. But before recounting them, he let Neill know he'd clerked for Attorney General Knox in the District of Columbia after law school.

"You don't say," Neill responded with a hint of mockery.

But Cooper sipped his coffee coolly. Then he spoke in a surprisingly authoritative tone. "The Departments of Justice and State insist you exercise extreme caution regarding Benjamin Neill."

"The *State* Department?" intoned Clark.

"I'll explain that shortly." Cooper eyed Marshal Neill, adding, "It's curious that you and the object of your inquiry share the same surname. Care to explain that?"

Neill ran his thumb along his drooping mustache, as if reacting to a bloody nose. "Oblige me by keeping to the subject," he answered. "Tell me all there is."

Cooper cleared his throat. "Very well. The brief starts on the 23rd of May, 1861. That day Benjamin Neill and two other runaway slaves seek sanctuary at Fortress Monroe, Virginia. The next morning a rebel courier arrives under a flag of truce with a request from Reb major John B. Cary for the immediate forfeiture of the runaways under the Fugitive Slave Law. But when Benjamin Butler, commander of the Union's Department of the Virginia, learns they've been used to erect the enemy's fortifications, he refuses the request, declaring them the 'contraband of war.'"

He took another sip of coffee. Had he observed Marshal Neill, instead, he might've detected a faint look of relief. Clark saw it. Then he rose from his chair, strutting before them as he spoke, gesticulating grandiloquently, his wristwatch glinting gold.

"In June 1861, Benjamin Neill volunteers for the 6th Colored Troops in which he serves with distinction through April 1864, when under heavy fire in the Battle of Deep Bottom, Virginia, he rescues his regimental colors from a fallen comrade. This act of bravery earns him the Congressional Medal of Honor and he is assigned to U.S. Grant's bodyguard."

This time Marshal Neill's reaction was impossible to miss: he twisted in his seat and grabbed hastily for his cup. Both Cooper and Clark watched him with some detachment. The grandfather clock's ticking seemed to grow louder.

"That was ages ago," Clark put in. "We'd like to know why the marshal can't—"

"Why he can't just run the Negro out of town?" He pointed a pink finger at Neill. "If you were wholly ignorant of his history, you wouldn't have sought direction from the Justice Department."

To Marshal Neill, Cooper was merely another cocky functionary. What kind of man wore a wristwatch, anyway? And Clark, with his fine liquors, fancy furniture, and newly fashionable cigarettes, was little better.

Neill stood up in disgust, thrust his hands into his pockets, and withdrew to the windows overlooking Capitol Park and its tall pines. His gaze dropped from the bristly, shimmering treetops to the lush grass and shade below. Another beautiful day in Cheyenne. People enjoying their easy city lives. "Save me the remarks," he muttered, turning back, "but keep on with the story."

Cooper slid again into his chair, perhaps cowed by Marshal Neill's hostile glare. "To many Negroes he's known simply as the *prophet* Benjamin, and over the past thirty years he's made quite a name for himself. Living amongst the northern colored elite after the war, he taught himself languages and even law and philosophy from books. A proponent of the so-called natural rights of human beings, he commonly quotes Rousseau in his sermons."

"Who?" asked Marshal Neill.

Cooper sighed with pity. "Jean Jacques Rousseau, eighteenth century French philosopher. Developed the principles of Natural Law—all men are created equal, and so forth. He helped inspire the French Revolution and his writings influenced our founding founders."

"So?"

"So the prophet Benjamin travels from town to town preaching Rousseau's values and declaiming on the subjugation of his race. He compares the continuing plight of the American Negro to the Jews' slavery in Egypt. He sings—yes, sings—to them about the promised land, the river Jordan, you get the idea. In the South he's stirred up Negro communities whose servitude arguably didn't end with the war between the states, it just assumed a different name—sharecropping. In him, his Negro audiences see a man who used his liberation to rise above his white oppressor, and not just in a moral or intellectual sense—his army service made him good with a gun. More on that to come."

* * *

About this time Benjamin awoke in worse pain and discomfort than the day before. Arduously, he rose from bed and squeezed into a robe that Sally had found for him. To the bathroom he brought his gun. Little did he know that today the din of voices issuing from downstairs was not one of inquisitive locals. This crowd was black. Some had arrived by surrey taxi from the Hillsdale depot where they'd stepped off the dawn train from Cheyenne, others yesterday had driven their own hitches down from the Laramie Mountains along Lodgepole Creek before heading north with sunup this morning.

The first to arrive, riding in a caravan from Hillsdale, had been directed to the S&S by a slack-jawed carpenter erecting a new town marker at the start of Main Street.

Sally was equally stunned when the Negro procession filed in through the cafe doors. But she was ever so gracious to her new guests who, for their part, seemed relieved to have found a welcoming business. Not surprisingly, her local customers were less agreeable than they'd been the previous day when it was only Benjamin they had to reckon with. This morning they hastily paid up and left as their numbers were quickly exceeded by the visitors. Her kitchen help was similarly anxious, yet none spoke of mutiny because they reckoned Sally would double their day's wages for not turning yellow. They were right.

By nine o'clock the crowd was becoming restless in their seats, worries and rumor making the circuit like hankies at a funeral. Where was the prophet Benjamin?—and was he still the man he had been?

* * *

At the Saloon, meanwhile, Klyde O'Brien was beset by a different sort of crowd.

"Fess up, Klyde!" bellowed the crotchety Jesse Larcan, seated opposite him, a ribbon of stringy white hair dangling beside his red, broken-veined cheek. "What in heck's going on? There's niggers all over town!"

Nobody but Larcan could lose his temper with O'Brien without suffering rebuke or worse. Larcan had the longest and most distinguished military record of anybody in town. As a youth he'd fought with General Sterling Price in Chihuahua and later as a captain under Price in the Confederate Army of the West. When Price and his surviving troops retired to Mexico to avoid surrender to the Union, Larcan resigned his commission, first returning to his family in the Territory of New Mexico, and later heading onward north. Since selling his claim and livestock to O'Brien some years back he'd mostly just passed the time offering his two cents in the cow camp whether the boys liked it or not.

Beside him slouched Jack Carvey, collared with a bloodstained neckerchief; next to Carvey sat an equally sullen Slim Barker; while standing away from their table, as if loathe to associate with them, was Kev Holt, sipping a cup of tea.

O'Brien leaned back in his chair, squeezing his hands into his pockets and allowing his belly to flop over his cowhide belt and silver buckle. He offered no response, but the growing lines in his leathery skin betrayed his vexation.

Larcan persisted with the subtlety of a seasoned cowpoke. "Blackies just ain't welcome here, Klyde! We gotta close down the Sun and Sagebrush—and quick."

O'Brien was firm. "Sally's place is paid for. I can't close it down."

"You mean you won't," Larcan snapped back. "And Jack's drubbin' will go unpunished. He was protecting your interests!"

"Whatever they are," Carvey added, sore-necked.

With his right hand, O'Brien rubbed the back of his own neck. "Fortunately he spared you, Jack."

Larcan scoffed. "We ought to compose a card of gratitude! 'Dear Negro Stranger, much obliged for sparing our partner, Jack.'"

O'Brien held his temper. "We'll wait for Marshal Neill."

"When's he gettin' back? Tonight? Tomorrow?"

"I expect a cable from him today."

"By then," Slim Barker ventured with careful prodding, "it could be too late."

"For what?" said Klyde. "Them Negroes ain't armed— on purpose, I reckon." He lowered his gaze and caressed his smooth scalp with the palm of his hand. Finally, "All right … kick up some dust getting over there," he said. "But don't go making a bad situation worse."

* * *

Back in Cheyenne, Attorney General Sam Clark was expressing his view that the Negro should never have been brought across the Atlantic, his cheeks flushed with conviction. "Granting them freedom was Lincoln's moral imperative, but what good is freedom to today's sharecropper? If a fresh and equal start is what they want, I say let them have it—back in Africa."

"President Lincoln proposed that very solution to Frederick Douglass, a friend and mentor of the prophet Benjamin," replied Cooper.

"I gather it wasn't favorably received." Clark extinguished his cigarette in the silver ashtray. "We've got a small colored population here in Cheyenne. Why hasn't this so-called prophet paid us a visit, Russ?"

"Maybe he has. That doesn't mean you or I would hear about it. Why don't you inquire with the Idelman whores? Maybe some of your prosperous Negro citizens give him handouts. Haul Barney Ford in here and ask if he's been putting him up at the Inter-Ocean. He might've slept there before heading north to chase Marshal Neill out of town."

"Beg your pardon?" Neill retorted from the windows. He'd been standing with his back to them.

"Old Barney won't talk," Clark cut in. "But pay a whore enough and she'll do practically anything." He slid a mischievous look at Marshal Neill. "Jim, how'd you like stopping by Idelman's tonight for me?"

Neill wasn't amused. "What about the gunfighting?"

Cooper nodded. "He's been tried for murder here and there after his presence sparked duels. In each case, white witnesses testified to his acting in self-defense."

"He wins friends among us, does he?" Clark responded. "Does the prophet Benjamin beguile our creamy skinned maidens too?" Succumbing to temptation, he reached again for the cigarette box. He lit up and crossed his legs.

Marshal Neill returned to his seat and hunched over his coffee cup. "What makes his preaching dangerous?"

"For one thing, Negro workers are vital to several major industries back East," replied Cooper. "And sharecropping constitutes an integral component of the southern economy, as slavery did before it. Stirring up discord amongst these people could threaten both industry and agriculture. And if they were to unite in a rebellion the security of the nation would be at risk."

"Surely he hasn't advocated insurrection," said Clark.

"I'm merely repeating the fears I heard voiced in Washington. Consider that the prophet Benjamin's influence extends beyond his own race to working men all over the county and common people from all over the world. You may be aware that nearly a million destitute foreigners immigrate each year. Even children work in the factories. We've all seen the Chinamen, the Mexicans, and the Negroes slaving away together on the railroad. He preaches to them, sings to them, builds their confidence and pride. To these people he's the embodiment of defiance and hope. And his appeal to intellectuals is just as profound—I know."

"Sounds like a socialist," said Clark.

"His party affiliation isn't known for certain. But he is indeed perceived as a natural voice for socialism in America—a champion of the common man."

"And the common woman too?" Clark snickered. "Jim, far as I know there isn't a single minority in your town except the odd Swede. No industry either. So why's he up there?"

"And why are you down here?" said Cooper.

Marshal Neill emptied his cup in a gulp. He rose with a grunt and retreated yet again to the towering panes of glass.

Clark and Cooper waited in vain for a response.

Cooper adjusted his cufflinks, then checked his sleeves for traces of lint. Finding a fleck, he flicked it away. "In 1895 it's discovered that a Pinkerton agent assigned to his surveillance, a certain...." Visibly critical he hadn't committed the name to memory, he shuffled through his stack of cablegrams. "Here it is ... it's discovered that a *Negro* agent named Ferdinand Schavers is using his access to Benjamin Neill to courier messages between him and a British socialist organization called the Fabian Society."

"I've met this Schavers," Clark realized, "a big, bearded man. President Lincoln's first bodyguard. He opened a hotel in Denver with Barney Ford and recently bought into the local Pinkerton office."

"A very useful friend to our itinerant preacher, then and now," replied Cooper. "Schavers attends Mr. Lincoln from 1861 to 1864 when he becomes a recruiting officer for the Indiana Colored Regiments. After the war he moves to Denver to work for the Pinkertons, no doubt because of his wartime connection with Allan Pinkerton himself."

Cooper drew a breath. He needed one. "The Justice Department uses Pinkerton detectives to monitor the prophet Benjamin's movements. Somehow it slips by that both men could've become acquainted during the war. Under this most convenient cover, Schavers links Benjamin Neill to the socialists abroad. As you know, Schavers is a notable man in his own right. He's written books about his times with both Lincoln and Pinkerton and once joined Frederick Douglass on a speaking tour of England and France. In '95 federal agents intercept a letter from the Fabians inviting the prophet Benjamin on a European speaking tour of his own. The letter is sent through Schavers and signed by George Bernard Shaw."

He hesitated, perhaps expecting Marshal Neill to ask, "Who?"—but this time Neill wouldn't afford him the satisfaction.

"The Pinkerton Agency," Cooper explained, "promptly reassigns Schavers, and at Justice's urging the State Department denies Benjamin Neill's passport application under Section Six of the Suspicious Activities Control Act."

"The *what?*" asked Neill.

"The Suspicious Activities Control Act of 1889, passed to quell the growing influence of both the Fabians and another

British organization, the Marxist Social Democratic Federation. The prophet Benjamin—"

"Quit calling him that—his name's Ben!" Neill stepped forward from the windows.

In a glance Cooper showed surprise to Clark, who leaned in to ask, "But why deny him a passport? With him overseas the State Department could deny him reentry."

"More grist for the mill!" said Cooper. "Yet another criticism of America to air from a rally in Trafalgar Square. But he wouldn't be the first Negro to criticize America from a British pulpit—the reverend Nathaniel Paul, William Wells Brown, Frederick Douglass all lectured in England about the continuing plight of their race. What makes Benjamin Neill different and perhaps more dangerous is that he appeals to *all* working men irrespective of color."

"And the educated kind like you," Neill grunted.

"Irrespective of color," Clark added with a grin.

Unfazed, Cooper shuffled through his cablegrams. "In 1897, having failed to overturn the passport denial in the Court of Appeals of the District of Columbia, Benjamin Neill's lawyer brings suit against the Secretary of State himself. But the U.S. District Court refuses to hear the case, claiming lack of jurisdiction. When his efforts finally make their way to the Supreme Court in 1900, the State Department explains its position with the following statement: 'The diplomatic embarrassment that could still arise from the presence of such a political meddler, traveling under the protection of an American passport, is easily imaginable.' The court rules that the Secretary of State had merely exercised his discretionary power to refuse a passport request from a person whose 'stated aims run contrary to the interests of the nation.' The State

Department tells the court it would review Benjamin Neill's case only after he acknowledges or renounces membership in the Socialist Party."

"Meanwhile he's at liberty to agitate in his own country—and in my town," Neill remarked, shaking his head.

"Well, he's an American, isn't he?" Cooper retorted. "While Washington has sought to limit his sphere of influence, it must also uphold his fundamental right to protest from our soil. And mindful of his vigilant friends at home and abroad its dealings with him must be defensible. Hence the insistence you restrain yourself, Marshal. If anything happens to Benjamin Neill, this very office would come under intense scrutiny from his powerful friends. Washington would be displeased."

"Woo-wee!" said Clark. "We certainly want to avoid that! Don't we, Jim?"

Marshal Neill helped himself to another cup of coffee at the wet bar, where the kettle sat on an electric burner. Pointing at the collection of bottles neatly arranged on the bar, he asked, "Mind if I add some fire to this?"

"You go right ahead," Clark answered sympathetically.

Neill laced his coffee with brandy and took a fragrant sip. He lingered there, staring down at the liquor bottles, his grey hair fallen in clumps over his brow. "There's four more years left of his story, Mr. Cooper," he said, "and you've sure got our attention...."

* * *

Stooping slightly in his slicker and his eyes mindful of each step, Benjamin cautiously descended the stairs into the dining hall. But when his sudden appearance elicited an explosion of applause from his followers he rose to his full height, and, registering the color of his audience, adopted a hero's pose with hands clasped above head. At once a dozen hollering men and women sprang from their seats, followed by another dozen. The thunderous acclamation swelled further when Benjamin held out his hands, palms down, and bowed his head, as if in blessing.

At this, Sally stepped deeper behind the bar.

Benjamin took his place before the crowd.

As the commotion subsided, he greeted his followers. "Ladies and gentlemen. Sisters and brothers! What a wonderful surprise. No doubt Barney Ford has spread the word from Cheyenne."

Explained one, "We met in the cellar of his hotel and decided to spread the word!"

Called another, "We've been awaiting your return!"

Another raised clasped hands. "Unity, brother!"

"Unity and dignity for all," Benjamin responded with a perfunctory nod. "But Barney shouldn't have gone shooting his mouth off. I'm not here to speechify. This time I'm on personal business."

Now an elderly woman expelled a throbbing cry: "You're a messenger, you are! A witness to the Good Lord!" Glancing this way and that, she asked, "Do I got a witness?"

"You got it!"

"Amen!"

Then she commenced to lead the crowd into song with the spiritual "I Want to be Ready to Walk in Jerusalem Just Like John."

From East to West Benjamin had received ecstatic exhortations with or without reference to the Creator—in meeting halls, churches, shipyards and foundries, outside mines, courthouses, factories and train depots, from far flung towns to scattered metropolises to dappled fields of cotton. For him these assemblies, big or small, fell into routine. In the past his ready perorations and responses were delivered with little physical or mental strain, and without any jitters; but today while his enraptured audience rejoiced in song he lowered his brow not in humility but in a gripping, lonely panic—like a runner poised at the starting line before an expectant crown, but questioning his abilities after a long convalescence. Finally, affording his followers a grateful if somewhat vacant smile, he balled a fist in solidarity.

Chapter Six

The townspeople, in a churning mass of shopkeepers, tradesmen, smallholders, clerks, and whole families, had gathered outside the Sun and Sagebrush Inn, while a cluster of cowpokes had summoned up the courage to steal onto the porch and peer through the windows at the animated Negro assembly. Jeannie McIntyre was among the spectators in the street. Flanked by her parents she shivered in the cold, wondering if David Cohen was in there with all those colored people, singing and shouting and stamping their feet. Jeannie crossed her arms to warm her hands. Her fair hair blew over her face. Behind her, two old biddies, their whispers segmented by the howling wind, exchanged remarks about Benjamin's politeness, his gentleness, his charm. Meantime, Mr. McIntyre's attention was divided between the armed men jostling for views through the windows and those struggling for space at the doorway. His pulsing cheek indicated grinding teeth, a sign of frustration he'd left his gun at home.

Now, only slightly restrained by the thin pine walls of the S&S, Benjamin's great baritone resounded in song throughout Main Street, carrying a melodious prayer not unlike a church hymn, but one whose haunting lament conveyed a message more and more threatening to the townspeople as it formed into a kind of battle cry: "*Good day to Thee, Lord God Almighty … here am I before Thee … with a solemn plea for this my people … what hast Thou done to this Thy people? … why hast Thou so oppressed this Thy people? … there is spite against the sons of oppressed! … on this earth how many nations? … the Romans, the Persians, the Babylonians … the Persians, what boast they? … our ruler is above all rulers! … the Romans, what boast they? … our kingdom is above all kingdoms! … and from my place I shall not move … I will not move from this place! … and an end let there be … to all this sorrow and suffering!*"

Then, in an exotic tongue only David might have known, Benjamin wailed an ancient prayer to exalt the dead, "*Yitgadal, veyitkadash, shmei raba!*"

Mrs. McIntyre craned her birdlike skull toward her attractive daughter. "See that nigger-loving Jew again and find your belongings in the street!"

As Jeannie's parents gravitated toward the inn with the crowd, the men itching their gun butts, she seized the opportunity to slip away.

In the loft above the stables, quite oblivious to the goings-on next door, David was reading on his sleeping mat, bootless but otherwise fully clothed under woolen sheets.

Having arisen before dawn, he'd finished his morning chores in record time, eager to return to last night's examination of David Walker's *Appeal to the Colored Peoples of America*. But the clanking of the door below now drew his attention. A distinctive series of sneezes provoked by a whiff of hay identified his caller. He pushed aside the book and coverings, slipped into his boots, and slid down the ladder.

His flush of excitement paled at the sight of Jeannie's disapproval. She shivered in a woolen coat glistening with precipitation.

"You got to stop all this, David." Her tone was sharp and definitive.

He stepped forward. "I'm not sure I understand, Jeannie. But remove that coat and let me throw a blanket around you."

She sneezed again, withdrawing. "Never mind that."

"But you're wet as a trout."

He came toward her and again she drew back, her expression resolute.

"David, you're going to ruin whatever chance we've got by keeping your present company. Sally Murphy's a bad influence. You'll get yourself run out of town."

Given his ignorance of the incident unfolding a stone's throw from them, David was perplexed. "I don't follow you, Jeannie. Does this concern Sally taking in a Negro boarder?"

But her mind was set on a quick—and potentially lifesaving—solution. "Go straight to Preacher O'Conner and request a baptism."

David threw up his hands. "What brung this on? Another attempt by your folks to ... to save me?"

Again he tried to approach her but she retreated step for step. He noticed tears in her eyes. Why would she not let him come near?

"David, you must accept Jesus ... or go somewhere else— for our sake and for your own safety."

"Accept Jesus *and* Klyde O'Brien, you mean. I reckon you've already arranged a Saloon job for me. A bit of Christian charity?"

"I was thinking of marshal's deputy—it's come time for one."

At first David's face flushed with amusement. "Jeannie, you done got it backwards—and I don't mean you should convert instead. Oh, I know I should go, I know I must go. But we could start out together, and start over someplace else, in a city, I mean. Maybe Denver, maybe out East." He stumbled forward with teary eyes, this time driving her against a Douglas fir column behind. When his hands fell on her shoulders she wrestled with him, bracing herself against the beam and pushing him away with surprising determination.

"Run away?" she wailed. "With you? My family's here!"

"Yeah? What kind of family? And what kind of life?" No wonder she wanted him to part from Sally's employ. His boss was the only person who truly accepted him for who he was—that is, until Benjamin came to town.

"Somebody round here needs a right whipping," she cried, "and it ain't me. For God's sake, he's only an old nigger!"

In the instant of silence that followed, David absorbed her anger and deduced the primary reason for her visit. Then he raised his hand and slapped her. The strength of the blow spun her around and against the pillar, which she clutched, sobbing, like a troubled child seeking sanctuary in her mother's indifferent embrace.

David offered a teary apology and sank to the floor.

After a minute of shared weeping, Jeannie turned herself around to face him. Leaning on the column and massaging her cheek, she said, "At least you're not in there with the rest of them."

David lifted his swollen eyes. "In there with who?"

"You mean you don't know what's happening?" she answered. "The inn's chock full of colored people."

* * *

Barricaded in the kitchen, Sally's helpers were contending for views into the dining hall, while behind the bar Sally had started on her second coffee and brandy. Benjamin, whose voice had been booming throughout the room in both song and speech, found himself interrupted mid-sentence when David threw open the rear door and bounded inside as if called to arms. Yet the sight of this Negro pilgrimage brought him to a stupefied halt. Benjamin responded by casting an arched eyebrow his way before returning to his audience. With the resumption of his oration, Sally motioned David to her side.

"Oh yes, brothers and sisters," Benjamin went on somberly, "I have experienced my share of injustices—and I've led a lonesome life because of the memories that haunt me and the defiance I am unable to restrain."

But now Benjamin was interrupted yet again.

Jack Carvey, Slim Barker, and Kev Holt pushed their way through the cowpokes jamming the doorway. The assembly stirred uncomfortably, their attention flitting back and forth between these armed strangers and their own stalwart champion. While the trio scanned the room, Benjamin resisted the urge to draw his concealed gun.

"Come for instruction?" asked Sally over the heads of the crowd. "Then join us. But your guns stay with me."

When after a moment's pause they didn't respond, she reached under the counter for Benjamin's Winchester.

"You," said Benjamin, pointing at Carvey. "I thought you weren't coming back."

Carvey untied his bloodstained neckerchief to reveal the gruesome marks of their encounter on the prairie. "I reckon I owe you somethin'," he replied.

"Indeed you do. You owe us all your respect," said Benjamin. "If you fancy taking another breath, forfeit your weapons. This instant."

Sally brought up the rifle and took aim, the crowd clearing a path and stepping away from her targets.

Carvey's upper lip trembled. Barker's eyelids narrowed. But Holt calmly unbuckled his gun belt and approached Sally through the interval that had opened between them. After exchanging urgent glances, his two partners followed his lead.

Surrendering his gun, Jack Carvey offered Sally his yellow smile. "Whiskey for me."

"In your face?"

Holt was the first to take a seat at the counter. There was a collective sigh from the crowd and a rustling among them as they shifted their bodies again toward Benjamin, who resumed his sermon in the heavy air of the room:

"After the founders of our country won independence from the British, they framed a constitution in accordance with the words of a French sage who proposed that Man and Woman should enjoy a basic right endowed by nature—a right to freedom."

"Amen to that!" snapped a stocky and mustached black cavalry sergeant as he parted the cowpokes plugging the doorway. Four plains troopers strutted inside after him. In their khaki summer service uniforms, wide-brimmed hats, and dusty knee-length boots, his subordinates shared his confident look. "Sergeant Terrence Briggs, 9th Cavalry out of Fort Russell," he said.

Looking somewhat annoyed by this further interruption, Benjamin nevertheless nodded respectfully. "What brings you to these parts, Sergeant Briggs?"

"En route to the Medicine Bow reserve. Come here first to survey the map with a rancher name of O'Brien. But finding you in the very same town, we thought to make a courtesy call first."

"How thoughtful," Benjamin responded with a curious air of detachment. "What's going on up there with the Cheyenne?"

"O'Brien's been granted grazing rights on Medicine Bow due to storm damage hereabouts. This morning we got a removal order from the General Land Office."

Benjamin grunted. "Just where are the Cheyenne headed now?"

"Thunder Basin."

"What a noble assignment, Sergeant Briggs!"

Before the affronted soldier could respond, Benjamin pressed on with his sermon.

"Though European nations were outlawing it," he said, "slavery continued to flourish in America. That much is obvious. But has it been suitably regarded that when Thomas Jefferson purchased the huge Louisiana territory from France he was faced with perhaps the greatest moral decision ever to confront a president?—to allow or prohibit slavery there. By contrast, General Washington had accepted leadership of a country in which human bondage was already widespread. As for Lincoln's famous Emancipation Proclamation—or should I call it infamous?—it applied only to rebel states over which he had no jurisdiction while exempting the neutral border states."

"Ain't that a fact!" someone cried.

Benjamin nodded, hands on hips. "Some good it did to pronounce free a Georgia cotton picker in the year 1863! By contrast, the Louisiana Purchase offered Jefferson a noble opportunity to make the country grow free. So how did freedom's framer act?"

"I get a feeling he's gonna tell us," Carvey groaned.

Benjamin paid him no mind. "Naturally in the interests of those with the labor force to cultivate the land rapidly! And the result? A bigger, stronger, more populous South that would later sustain an armed rebellion over so-called State's Rights—or the right to own human chattel—at the cost of more than half a million lives. Finally, with the collapse of the rebellion arose the problem of what to do with over one million newly freed men and women. The handy economic solution of which we're all too familiar was sharecropping —or slavery by a different name."

"So it is," agreed someone else.

"In 1870 the 15th Amendment did little in actual terms to raise our people up," Benjamin continued, "and to this day our southern brothers and sisters are still virtually enslaved and subject to unchecked racial violence. In the last quarter-century two thousand have lost their lives to southern lynching mobs. Not fifty or a hundred and fifty, but two thousand! Hence, many of us, not just for better economic conditions, but to protect our very lives, have migrated north and west. Yet true equality remains unattained. Besides the all-Negro community of Deerfield in Colorado, and a few others like it, throughout the rest of the country our subject status remains. What else but indignation over our continuing plight has brought you here today?"

With his listeners absorbed again by his peroration, Benjamin was now deftly stoking their fire.

Leaning across the bar, Jack Carvey had to repeat Sally's name twice before gaining her attention. "How come they get to keep their weapons?" he whispered, nodding toward the soldiers.

"Oh, shut your lid, Jack," she responded.

"Can't say I fancy being subject to a darky's gun."

"I reckon you should be growing accustomed to it. That's twice in as many days."

Carvey colored.

Barker snorted laughter while Holt allowed himself a smirk at Carvey's expense.

Heedlessly, Benjamin proceeded in his speech: "The framers of the Constitution hardly had our interests in mind when they designed a representational democracy favoring the landowners—not the land *workers*—who built this country. Thus, in the first protest book of our people, back in 1829, Mr. David Walker wrote, 'America is more our country than it is the whites'…. The greatest riches in all America have risen from our blood and tears.' And yet a high fence still separates us from the groves of sundry fruits of our own planting."

Benjamin lifted his big fist. "Against this obstacle, let us raise our picks and axes!"

His listeners rose to their feet, knocking over chairs, applauding, whistling and crying out, and generally causing the Sun and Sagebrush Inn to shudder on its foundations.

In the midst of this sudden clamor, their defender doubled over in a series of violent coughs, but as concern for him began to diminish the excitement, he stood tall and thrust a finger at the O'Brien boys.

"*They* will try to deny us what is rightfully ours. They may even try to kill us. But we must not waver in our demand for *full* citizen's rights—by our deeds shall we be known, and by their deeds shall we know them!"

From the crowd arose a fresh hysteria.

Finding themselves the objects of the assembly's agitation, Carvey, Barker, and Holt abandoned their seats in such haste they left their guns behind with Sally, pushing through the clustered bodies and propelling themselves out the swinging doors. A wave of mocking laughter rolled through the crowd. Benjamin tried to regain command of his audience with useless calls for quiet.

Sally meantime availed herself of the chance to splash more brandy into her mug.

At last Benjamin succeeded in restoring order, and while his listeners were reclaiming their seats he made a plea on their hostess' behalf for lasting calm. Then, as he bolstered himself for the remainder of his stump speech, Sergeant Briggs confronted him with what began as a rudimentary— and manageable—challenge:

"You give a mighty lecture," he said, "but progress requires our working with the white man, not causing trouble."

Benjamin's thunderous response was automatic.

"Work with him or *for* him? And to what ends in your case? To remove Indians permanently because of a mere change in the weather?"

The intensity of his retort brought on another grim fit of coughing. Once more he doubled over.

Sergeant Briggs exploited Benjamin's brief incapacity to launch his defense—yet in a tone so high his voice cracked. "My daddy died a slave and I was born one. But I'm proud to serve in the United States Cavalry. Why shouldn't I serve my country? Our ranks helped free the slaves. And just six years ago it was our 10th Cavalry that saved Teddy Roosevelt at Kettle Hill."

Benjamin drew a breath. "And it was the 9th and 10th Cavalries that removed the Comanche, the Kiowa, the Apache, and—just where should I stop, Sergeant?"

Jacking his spine, Briggs responded, "I might not agree with every assignment, but for my service I'm respected by the army. And that's good for our people."

Recovering himself, Benjamin delivered his response: "You reckon you enjoy the respect of the federal government? Well, let me ask you this, Sergeant Briggs. If you had the courage to resign your position in protest—in protest of being charged with oppressing your Indian brothers and sisters—who do you suppose would replace you?"

"Suppose I did walk away? Suppose I up and left a job with prestige and the promise of a pension. What good would it do? Somebody else would take my place. My quitting won't help."

"As a soldier I once shared your view. But you didn't answer my question. Just who would replace you?"

"Another soldier...."

"What kind of soldier, Sergeant Briggs?"

"One of my men, I suspect."

"But not a white man."

"Ain't likely."

"Have you ever wondered why not a white cavalry officer?"

All attention was on Sergeant Briggs.

"Well, at the rank of sergeant, I don't suppose his color would match troop!" He grinned self-satisfactorily at his men.

"*Terrence Briggs*," Benjamin called. "Instead of soiling his own hands, the cunning white man throws *us* the dirty jobs like bones to hungry dogs. Thus the good ol' boys in Washington pit one colored people against another. They mock us, Sergeant Briggs, while sipping cognac in their wood-paneled offices. In the war between the states we were paid just ten dollars a week. Yet for our brave service—and I know this because I was there—our superiors awarded us with the honorifics Nigger Tom, Nigger Joe, and *Nigger Ben*."

Then Benjamin expressed one of his most controversial opinions, particularly among his own people, many of whom, like himself and Sergeant Briggs, had sought to prove their worth through soldiery: "It has therefore become my contention that until our people can stand in full human dignity as Americans we should not bear America's arms."

The shutters outside trembled in a powerful gust.

Among the crowd whispers were exchanged. After a moment Sergeant Briggs snapped, "That ain't no solution! My quitting won't help me, it won't help our people, and it won't help our country."

"Here-here!" responded his troops, followed by some "amens" from the general rumble of the audience.

"Our people and our country need leadership by example!" Benjamin countered.

"At what cost?" Briggs responded. "Take yourself. What've you got for your sacrifices except some friends and foes? And what've you got us? Maybe our grandchildren will benefit from men of your bravery and sacrifice—but for us *right now* positions like yours do more harm than good."

Sergeant Briggs had struck him where he was weakest—on a personal point, a point of judgment. But Benjamin was careful not to cede control of the occasion by defending himself. Instead, he tried to slip away from his rival's clutches without showing distress. Addressing the whole crowd, not Briggs alone, he modified his message and tone accordingly: "Among my rewards are many dear relationships with white folks who have made their own sacrifices for our cause, and for causes aligned with ours for which we work together in this country and abroad."

He gestured toward Sally and David. "It takes more guts and more conviction to stick your neck out for an unpopular principle than merely to sign up and serve. That's leadership by example. And we Negroes must acknowledge that for every one of us there's a white person who would come to our rescue, one who would fight at our side for justice."

Unwittingly Benjamin had given Sergeant Briggs another opportunity to strike:

"Yet we should show our gratitude by refusing to defend them in war?"

With a pendulous swing of his chin Benjamin could be seen absorbing the blow with marked vexation. But he would not be felled. He had learned to dismiss exercises of logic that interfered with his defiant emotional positions.

In any case, he was too close to the end of his speech—and his stamina—to be dragged into a quarrel. "No matter how intense our trials," he went on, "we must keep our faith in those like Sally and David here, for if they love us we shall eventually gain full citizen's rights and the acceptance of the greater society."

Now, his voice faint, he confessed, "At times even I have gone astray feeling my work is in vain. And once I allowed self-pity to nearly put out my light." With his palms open toward the ceiling he raised his hands as if to lift the spirits of his audience with them, but a keen eye might have noticed that his left wrist was crossed with scars. "Yet it has always been people like Sally and David who have restored my faith in the oneness of people."

Then with clenched fists, he thundered, "*Together* we must build a home in this rock, the rock of America!"

Rather than provoking another round of commotion, at this juncture silence prevailed save the shutters rattling in the wind.

David ended the hush by calling out the words "*Bye and bye*" in song.

Faces in the crowd lifted.

Sally gave him a stunned look over her shoulder.

Benjamin reacted with a smile before he repeated David's words in a lower note, followed by the continuing verse, "*I'm gonna lay down this heavy load.*"

David called out another "*bye and bye*" in the higher note and again Benjamin responded with "*bye and bye,* I'm gonna lay down this heavy load" in the lower one.

David continued singing: "*Oh when I get to heaven gonna sing and shout …*"

And Benjamin joined in harmony: *"I'm gonna lay down this heavy load …"*

"There's nobody there to turn me out …"
"I'm gonna lay down this heavy load …"
"Oh bye and bye …"
"Bye and bye, I'm gonna lay down this heavy load …"

The crowd joined in with the next verse, rising together as though by signal. Even the soldiers, standing in back, contributed their voices. Somebody began playing along on the decrepit and off-key piano, and after the last harmonizing notes had been held by those singing along, Sally noticed Terrence Briggs sitting quietly at the keyboard.

A short while later, Benjamin repeated his call for solidarity and wished his followers a safe journey home. In the drizzle outside, the townspeople gave the departing crowd a wide berth. Sergeant Briggs and his men stayed behind to exchange goodbyes with Benjamin.

But Benjamin's first action was to approach Sally at the bar and express his gratitude. Next, he turned glowingly toward David. But the boy's gaze was stuck on the batwing doors. Something was wrong.

* * *

Sam Clark extinguished the butt of another cigarette. "Russ, before the marshal joined us this morning you alluded to Benjamin Neill's declining health."

"More like a collapse," Cooper responded from his seat at the end of the coffee table. "Years of confinement and court battles have taken their toll. Even so, until October

1900 he'd campaigned vigorously for his right to travel. The British paid the legal fees and in London they rallied with banners emblazoned with the demand *Free Benjamin Neill*. But since the rejection of his appeal to the Supreme Court the Fabians would seem to have forgotten him. Worse, the increasingly incendiary views he expressed during this desperate period, such as that Negroes shouldn't serve in the armed forces, led to his alienation by colored groups formerly allied with him."

"Fascinating," Clark remarked.

"Quite." Cooper held a glint in his eyes. "Fearing repercussions, prominent members of the black intelligentsia placed disclaimers in some of the eastern papers. I recall seeing one with the caption, *Benjamin Neill Does Not Speak for the Negro People*."

The clock struck ten.

"With their support withdrawn," Cooper concluded, "he found himself relegated to the fringes of the movement. Most public venues closed their doors to him, even the press tired of him. Finally, Pinkerton agents began to report a noticeable loss of vigor."

"How much longer can he keep at it?" asked Clark. "He must be in his sixties."

"And in poor health," Cooper added. "In these records I can find no reference to a family."

Marshal Neill took a definitive gulp of his spiked coffee. "Well … I best be going."

But Cooper wasn't finished. "At Yale we studied his clashes with the government—which were, it begs mentioning, the subject of much debate on constitutional grounds. I'd enjoy meeting him for myself."

Marshal Neill didn't hide his disdain. "I reckon he'd be honored to make *your* acquaintance." He drained his cup and reached for his Stetson on the rack by the door.

Rising from his seat, Clark eyed Marshal Neill. "Is there anything you wish to tell us, Jim? Anything that could make a difference?"

Marshal Neill felt as if his problems had been sensationalized as a means to boast the heroics of his adversary, but mainly his mind was back in town—his now tainted town.

"I take it you're in danger, Jim."

Marshal Neill's set-back eyes seemed even more remote. "It's an old debt," he muttered with almost paralytic resignation. "I always knew he'd come to collect someday. He ain't got much left to lose now, does he?"

Neill reached for the doorknob. "Much obliged, gentlemen."

As he stepped into the corridor Clark beckoned him.

The marshal leaned back inside. "Yeah, Sam?"

"My young-uns expect to see you at Frontier Day."

After a reflective pause Neill nodded and was gone.

Clark pondered his abrupt departure before transferring his attention back to Russ Cooper. "Now, tell me about *James* Neill…."

From the capitol Marshal Neill went to the office of the Postal Telegraph-Cable Company. He sent a message to O'Brien: "Do nothing in my absence. Collect me Hillsdale depot pm."

* * *

Something had happened outside the Sun and Sagebrush Inn, reversing the line of departing people and causing them to stumble back inside, tripping on each other's heels. Both Benjamin and Sergeant Briggs started immediately for the entrance followed closely by Briggs' men, and behind them David.

"Don't forget your sling!" Sally cried, waving Benjamin's gun belt in the air.

But he and Briggs were already fighting the current of retreating bodies.

At last they saw what awaited them in Main Street.

In the driving rain, a large force of mounted cowboys had formed in a crescent three riders deep, opposite the inn. Back of them, the townspeople in a diffuse mob were urgently retiring into the nearest shops.

Benjamin spotted O'Brien atop a palomino, center, fingering the trigger of his gigantic buffalo rifle. Behind him, Carvey, Barker, and Holt sat atop their horses grasping repeating rifles, replacements for their lost short guns.

Benjamin motioned with his hand for the troops to fall back to their horses tethered outside the inn. "Let's try to avoid a general engagement, shall we, Sergeant Briggs?"

Briggs assented with a reluctant nod. "Just remember to duck."

Then Benjamin lumbered out into the middle of the street and faced his old nemesis.

O'Brien wore a calfskin coat and a wide rain-spotted hat with a tilted brim, his red scarf flapping in the wind. His bushy eyebrows arched downward to form a threatening *V.*

Next to Benjamin appeared David, bearing the Winchester. Gaining confidence behind them, the cautious Negro travelers reemerged in a trickle from the S&S.

"They're leaving, Mr. O'Brien," David announced in a conclusive tone far exceeding his station.

Benjamin turned, noticing the firearm. "Watch it, now," he cautioned.

"Nigger and Jew make tarnation stew," O'Brien jeered. His palomino snorted and bobbed its head.

David ignored the taunt. "Let 'em go—without trouble, Mr. O'Brien. What would Marshal Neill say?"

Acknowledging his own negligence, Klyde replied, "They ought not been let in. Marshal Neill woulda met 'em at the city limits."

"Yeah," Jesse Larcan retorted with some belligerence, "just like he met the first nigger there."

"Let these people go, Mr. O'Brien. Best for everybody."

"*Let* them go? Do you reckon I want to keep 'em hostage? Troublemakers ought to be run out of town—and my boys here are expert drivers."

"Step down off that horse and let's see who does the running," said David.

Benjamin suddenly clutched him by the arm.

Klyde laughed a too-hearty laugh. His men remained rigid in their saddles but their horses, perhaps sensing the common anxiety, began shifting their weight. Was it the air of danger or merely the thrashing wind? Just then, a rider whose mount bore the markings of the U.S. Postal Service broke into the center of the human ring formed in the street, and, spotting O'Brien, delivered Marshal Neill's cablegram.

After snatching the message and giving it a cursory glance, Klyde told David, "I wouldn't even squander spit on you, Jew. Marshal Neill will hand down your punishment himself." He shook the cable in the air, drenching it.

"Sure, Mr. O'Brien. Marshal Neill ain't your slave. He's the law."

"Wise up, boy. Or find yourself in an early grave."

With that, Benjamin shoved his hands into his coat pockets and turned his back on O'Brien, dismissing his threat as idle—or expired. He faced his people, who formed half of the tense circle.

"On your way, dear friends. Do not fear for yourselves." He swung an open hand toward Sergeant Briggs. "Your way is safeguarded by the very men assigned to advance this bad man's interests."

"No doubt about that!" said Briggs. "The first part, I mean. Our mission has changed." He and his men untied their horses and regained their mounts in unison. O'Brien appraised them, creases like pincers appearing from his nose to his chin. Briggs trotted his horse into the middle of Main Street and caught O'Brien's wavering eye. "That's right, old man. We ain't doing your bidding—sure not after this."

"Enjoy your little rebellion while it lasts," O'Brien responded with a sly smile. "You're all headed for dishonorable discharge."

Briggs reined his horse to Benjamin who had remained in the street with his fists dug into his pockets.

"You offended my men back there," said Briggs. "To that, and to some of your views, I take exception. But I still hold my admiration for a man who has given—and given up—so much for his country and for his people." Now he fixed O'Brien with a conclusive hostile glare. "What've *you* done for our country? This man holds the Medal of Bravery."

He tipped his hat to Benjamin and swung his horse toward the group he would lead unmolested out of town.

Chapter Seven

That afternoon the town locksmith was open for business with a pot of hot cider brewing for the procession of customers he expected, but nobody so much as appeared on Main Street except the sentries O'Brien had posted every fifty yards. The locksmith soon abandoned his lofty ambitions and instead spiked the pot with a bottle of sour mash for those windswept men, who, after leaving their posts one at a time to partake of the brew, also took turns hosing down the prairie with it—as if the sodden plain could benefit from their solemn hydrate-and-irrigate ritual.

As O'Brien's best were thus drinking up and pissing away their morning Benjamin and David had withdrawn temporarily from the eye of the storm, riding shoulder to shoulder southwest of town. They had slipped out unnoticed by all but Kev Holt who shadowed them at a distance atop his roan.

"Don't know who he is," said David, responding to Benjamin having inquired about Holt. "Showed up in town a few days ago. Not like O'Brien's usual hog heads."

"Nor the type that makes his living cowpunching," Benjamin observed. "He's obviously a hired gun—not a hired hand."

"The kind with no backside."

"Yet he turned tail this morning and skedaddled ... all too eagerly, it seemed to me. No practiced gun would've fled. Yet he is practiced, I'm sure of that."

"Their leaving was a worse sign than their coming."

Benjamin nodded. "That's when I began to fear the outcome too. If not for the presence of the cavalry...."

"Maybe. But it wasn't just the cavalry that cocked me up. I felt strong at your side."

"I'm grateful for your show of loyalty back there. But defending me isn't worth your life. Don't risk it again."

David shrugged. "Marshal Neill won't let anything happen to me."

"You have faith in him. Why?"

"We got a special kind of friendship. He has no children and I have no parents."

Benjamin considered this, deeply. "Your marshal interests me. I'm eager to meet him tomorrow."

"A sort of reunion?"

"Forty years on."

"It sure must be important. Why'd you wait so long?"

Benjamin said nothing.

"Do you aim to take him away from me? That would be the end of our friendship too."

Benjamin turned with a smile. "Ours? Oh, I wouldn't like to lose that."

"You know," said David, "there's something very true about you when you ain't preaching."

Benjamin laughed, precipitating a short fit of gagging. "Really!" he managed to say at last. "My speechifying this morning seemed bereft of honesty?"

"Sure was a dandy performance. When you was trumpeting in there I saw a different man than I see now. I like this one a lot more."

"To them I'm a *public* figure. When they assemble as an audience, I must, with increasing reluctance, fit into my threadbare dancing shoes and sing the old songs. That's what they expect."

"That all you got left?"

But Benjamin did not respond.

"What about family, friends?"

"I have friends across this nation and across the world. Some I know only through impassioned correspondence. But I have no family. Your marshal had something to do with that. Something," he repeated.

David watched him gaze over the desolate terrain. A cold wind was rising. If Benjamin thought his shabby life should end in—or from—a confrontation with Marshal Neill, David reckoned there was no stopping him.

With a random scattering of grey whiskers poking through his parched face, Benjamin's skin resembled soil scorched by brushfire and strewn with ashes.

Benjamin abruptly halted his stallion with a chink of the bridle and a peal of leather.

Reigning his mare, David twisted in his saddle to make sure Holt stopped too. Next the boy revisited the dark profile over his shoulder.

While he surveyed their desolate surroundings Benjamin said as if in a trance, "That French philosopher, Rousseau ... he argued that because we populate the state and the land sustains us, nations should exist for the well-being of all—a self-evident proposition that both our country and his have failed to realize despite our outwardly democratic revolutions." Then, emerging from his enchantment, he transferred his attention to the young rider abreast of him. "Rousseau also contended that societies are shaped and governed by a general will. In the case of your town and others like it, that *will* goes against the fundamental rights of those like you and me."

"So why don't you advocate we stick around to change people's minds?"

"I prefer to go out in a blaze of gunfire," he answered matter-of-factly, "not strung up by the neck. And if you remain after I'm gone, you'll find yourself swinging or trampled on. Guess who'll come after you? It won't be Klyde O'Brien. You're a mere flapjack to him." He shook his finger at David. "It'll be your girl's father to save face. When we get back, you ought to acquire that there horse from Sally and pack your bags or you won't live to enjoy your liberation. It's not enough to get free of your shackles, sometimes you must simply *run*. I myself took to my heels long ago when the opportunity arose. At least get as far as Cheyenne or Denver where you'll find Jewish families eager to help."

David found the idea of real appeal. It was as if Benjamin had torn his life from its fixings by the roots and David was now free to plant himself anywhere. With this new horizon glowing in his mind he felt not the slightest reluctance to accept its beacon. But first he must make his boldest show yet of oneness with his savior.

Late that afternoon Marshal Neill stepped off the Cheyenne-Lodge Pole Express at Hillsdale where he was greeted by much hat-tipping and curtsying by locals awaiting other commuters from the capital. There to collect him were O'Brien, Jesse Larcan, and the town churchman, O'Conner. During the hour's carriage ride home, Larcan related the events of the past two days. O'Brien mostly just nodded his head. Marshal Neill, in turn, recounted what he'd learned in Cheyenne and agreed to a meeting later at the Saloon to decide how the law would respond to Benjamin Neill. O'Brien was eager to introduce the marshal to the promising Kev Holt. Preacher O'Conner, who doubled as the proprietor of the Mercantile, gave his blessing to any course of action that would both restore harmony to his parish and traffic to his shop. In this way he smartly avoided further involvement.

* * *

Coursing from Benjamin's room like a river of caramel through the inn's shadowy spaces, his gentle baritone carried a favorite hymn whose chorus went, *Nobody knows the trouble I've seen, nobody knows my sorrow,* while at the bar downstairs Sally absorbed every line, a shot of brandy her companion. Minutes before, she had locked up resignedly after the inn's first dead day in four years of operation. Among the worries occupying her mind was if her business could recover from her acceptance of Benjamin and his followers, yet she found herself less concerned about her own sacrifices than the peril that Benjamin and David now faced jointly. As for the dangers of her personal alliance with Benjamin, she was confident Marshal Neill would intervene on her behalf with Klyde O'Brien.

After a tiring day she gladly pulled the pins from the bun behind her ears and let down her hair. She kicked off her boots, unbuttoned the top buttons of her blouse, slackened her belt in the loops of her skirt, and took another reassuring sip of brandy.

Now the sounds of a new song began to spill downstairs in velvety sheets—*Sometimes I feel discouraged and think my work's in vain, but then the Holy Spirit revives my soul again*—and as she gazed into the depths of her drink, tears trickled down her face. No husband, no children, no hope of a proper woman's kind of life, and today her business in jeopardy. Maybe she should heed her widowed mother's calls to come home to Cheyenne where her sisters were both raising children to whom she could be a closer and more gratified aunt. Her contemplation finally led her to recall her lengthy and unsatisfied love affair with Marshal Neill, who shared her risk of growing old alone.

They'd first met back in '99 when she was working the concessions counter at Cheyenne's Frontier Day, and it wasn't long before he negotiated excellent terms with Klyde O'Brien for her purchase of the S&S plot. Neill himself had put up much of the inn's investment capital from his own holdings and when their passion wore out he merely wrote off the loss with a wistful smile.

So engrossing were her thoughts that she failed to notice the expiration of Benjamin's singing—until a calloused finger glided across her cheek and smoothed over her tears. Recognizing the scent of the man behind her, she did not recoil; instead, as her caresser's palms warmly cupped her face, she set aside the glass in her grasp and placed her hands on his, guiding them over her jaw, down her neck, and finally over her bosom. Then, pivoting in her seat, she curled her arms around Benjamin's shoulders and pressed her moist cheek against the base of his neck.

* * *

A persistent moon, now and again obstructed by drifting clouds, cast a variable glow onto the prairie—enough to light David's way as he again withdrew from town, this time on foot. When he paused to tighten his scarf not a sound greeted him, the crickets feeling the chill too. Here, alone with the impartiality of the plain, his mind was always at ease. And here, this night, he pondered Benjamin's madness. Recalling his statement that Negroes should not bear arms for their country, David marveled at how Benjamin could demand equality for his people and yet advocate a form of defiance sure to upset not only whites but blacks too, as he had seen for himself. Yet Benjamin's noble dedication to improving his country made him a better moral exemplar than those previous objects of David's veneration—his father and Marshal Neill. For what by contrast had he learned of leadership from them? And what was David himself but a coward beside such dignity and such courage?—he, who'd once considered starting over somewhere as a *Cohan* rather than a Cohen. This sudden self-awareness, along with his new respect for the Negro people, resounded like a bugle cry throughout his consciousness, and in the bracing blackness of the night he conceived a plan to preserve the life of the fullest man he had ever known.

When his plot had formed sufficiently in his mind he started back for town, breathing hard and hearing each breath as he drove himself over the brittle prairie grass. First he went to his room in the loft above the stables. Waiting in a dresser drawer was a small lacquered case he had carefully stowed away. With trembling fingers he opened it. Inside was his mother's golden *chai*—a symbol of his people recognized by Benjamin two days before in the photograph of David's parents. He lifted the delicate chain and for the very first time hung it about his own neck. Next he made his way to the rear door of the S&S, and, after using his passkey, tiptoed behind the bar where he switched on the electrical light. Reaching under the bar, he retrieved the pile of gun belts abandoned the previous day by O'Brien's boys.

He carefully rolled the coils out on the counter, sliding Sally's empty snifter out of the way. His next move was toward the gleaming tap from which he pulled himself a tall draught of beer.

Then he set to work.

* * *

Upstairs in the firelight's glow Sally and Benjamin embraced beside his bed. She unbuttoned his shirt to the waist and ran her hands down the length of his chest, eliciting a patch of goose bumps wherever her touch strayed. Her exploration continued around to his back, where she hesitated at the ribbing of thick scars. He reacted by recovering her hands and consuming them in his grasp. Now, having drawn her attention away from what had been done to him, he emphasized what he himself had done to others.

"Sally, I've killed with these hands ... many times...."

"And loved with them few?"

She wrapped her arms around his waist and peered into the shadowed spots below his brow. Finally, she pulled him close and let her eyes shut.

* * *

With the three gun belts slung over his shoulders and his hands shoved into the pockets of his denim jacket, David Cohen marched up darkness-drenched Main Street. He carried no gun of his own. His destination was marked by the huge stained-glass windows of Klyde's Saloon which threw a pattern of yellow and red light into the street. As he stepped into the glow he was spotted from beyond the Saloon by one of O'Brien's mounted sentries, who ordered him to stop. When David did not respond the sentry spurred his horse forward.

Heedless of the hoofbeats behind him, David ascended the steps to the Saloon until he reached what would prove the portal of his fate. He pounded on the wooden gate closed over the saloon doors but not yet padlocked. In a moment it swung forth and in the gap stood the craggy figure of Jesse Larcan. Remnants of dinner clung to his wiry beard—mashed potato from the looks of it. Just then the sentry rode up wildly but drew rein at Larcan's insistence, steadying his long gun nonetheless.

"Now what, Mr. *Co-han?*" Larcan nodded at the gun belts. "Hawking firearms?"

"Seeing as your associates left them when they run off, I offer them back at no charge."

Larcan's lips flipped from frown to smile. "In that case, howdy!"

Klyde's Saloon was a terrific sight. A giant statue of a naked female carved from redwood towered over the bar, her arms outstretched in welcoming fashion like the goddess of some ancient shrine. She divided two tall mirrors which together ran the entire length of the forty-foot counter. At her feet sat an oversized cash register plated with imitation gold. Against the mirror to the right leaned a framed magazine print of a bearded rogue offering a drink to a gentleman in a top hat—its title, *Stranger, Do You Irrigate?* Tacked over the racy statue's pubic mound was a caricature of a drink-wielding Carrie Nation entitled *Carrying the Nation!*

Opposite the bar ran three lines of round card tables that went from the entrance to the billiards area in back, where Kev Holt was playing against himself. To David's right stood an automatic playing piano on wheels with an exquisite stained-glass veneer.

A sullen Marshal Neill was seated with O'Brien, Carvey, and Barker at a table blanketed by O'Brien's cigar smoke. Before them was an array of half-empty bottles and glasses. The four men appeared like dwarfs in the vast cavern of the place, and in its cloudy chandelier light the marshal gave David a cautious nod. Holt, for his part, at first interrupted his game with no more than a cursory look over his shoulder; but when he recognized his own gun belt slung over the boy's shoulder he parted from his billiards stick.

O'Brien leaned back in his squeaky chair, brandishing his fat cigar. Its smoke tickled David's nostrils as he brought down the firearms on the closest table. Hungry for their weapons, Carvey and Barker rose together and made their way over to David. After fastening their slings about their waists with obvious relief, they gave him looks up and down that caused him to shift his weight. Then they stepped back, and with their palms hovering over their gun butts, they struck poses reminiscent of a Sears catalogue illustration for cowboy attire. Next, Holt approached David with an air of resignation, even—was it?—shame. After casting David a suspicious glance he pulled his revolver from its holster and flipped open the cylinder. Satisfied, he returned to his solitary game of billiards.

"Well, how about inspecting *your* guns?" O'Brien bellowed at the other two before sucking his cigar.

Carvey and Barker's quick verifications were rewarded with studded rings of gleaming lead which they showed triumphantly to their boss. Marshal Neill did not react to any of this. The undivided attention he gave David was like that of a concerned guardian. As for O'Brien, hardly paternal about the young Jew, he expelled a laterally rolling stream of smoke as if it was reminiscent of the conflagration that consumed the great Temple of Jerusalem.

A feeling of inevitability seized David and instead of withdrawing he stood his ground. He gave the whole bunch his ever more critical eye. In front of him were Carvey and Barker, poised to act on O'Brien's whim like a pair of dedicated dogs. Behind them was Larcan, now perched observantly on a barstool. Right of him were the seated O'Brien and Marshal Neill. Further to the right was Holt, waxing his billiards stick.

David set his jaw and stepped forward.

Carvey and Barker immediately closed ranks.

The youth did not show his fear. "You going to shoot a defenseless man?"

Carvey and Barker held their positions.

"By my estimation you ain't yet man-grown," O'Brien answered. "Let 'im come if he wants to grow up fast!"

David pushed Carvey and Barker apart and they gloweringly yielded to him. He halted at Neill's chair. "Fairness has always ruled with you, Marshal. But, if I may be so bold, this time you should've hung your hat at the S&S instead."

Neill's uncomfortable gaze fleetingly met his own.

O'Brien belched a single hoot, which Carvey and Barker took as a signal to belly laugh. Holt remained distant.

"You do plan to settle this peacefully, don't you, Marshal?"

Silence ensued.

David summoned up even more courage. "Marshal," he said, "you ain't taking their side without first letting Sally explain hers?" Unable to elicit a response, he added, "That's real disappointing. Don't look to me like any of these gentlemen is worth the sacrifice of your principles. But mine's a biased eye."

Without any movement from his frame, Marshal Neill's solemn gaze shifted from face to face.

"Makes you wonder if somebody's fearful of somebody," David went on, "or fearful of something that might get out if he talks things over instead of pushing lead."

Now Marshal Neill's brow furled. He intoned, "David, you best turn tail."

"Who says? You? Or your master?"

As if from a sudden stench, Neill's pudgy nose creased in on itself. The muscles in his cheeks and jaw labored like a nervous prairie rat's. Now he got to his feet and his steely eyes ordered David out.

"Away, Jew!" O'Brien bellowed. "We'll continue your schooling another day."

But David remained where he was.

"I said *get!* And you'd be smart to get out for good—for everybody's good."

When David didn't budge, O'Brien went on: "But if it's a martyr you wanna be, I'll gladly oblige. I'll jerk you both up a tree!"

David couldn't be bothered by the predictable Klyde O'Brien. Marshal Neill, on the other hand, had surprised and disappointed him.

"Where's *my* James Neill?" he continued, choking up. "Where's the man who helped dig my father's grave, who taught me how to shoot game? Where's the man who cooked me dinner once, and who invited me to Sunday brunch? Why, I remember how you refused my help when that egg split on the kitchen floor and you got down on your hands and knees to sop it up. Where is that man, Marshal? The one I see sitting right there in your chair ain't him. I see somebody else, somebody who looks the other way— somebody who answers to a bad man's call."

At this O'Brien rose from his chair and with a broad swing of his arm struck David on the shoulder with his cigar, sending ashes flying. Proving that O'Brien held all the actual authority there, Neill, with embers glowing on his own shoulder, did no more than block David's way. The boy stepped forward. Neill grabbed him by the arm, his grip so strong he initially succeeded at turning David toward the door, but that action put the two alongside each other, making it easy for David to shake off his hold and pivot toward O'Brien, eager for a fight.

The two collided among the card tables.

Ignoring Neill's order to stop, David struck first with a blow of such speed Neill was unable to thwart it. O'Brien cried out as he toppled sideways, his shattered nose spraying blood across the table over which he promptly tumbled. Its legs gave way and his massive form crashed to the floor.

Beatrice O'Brien now burst from the kitchen, throwing aside a stained apron and rushing to her husband's side.

Stunned by the success of his strike, David drew back, affording Neill a chance to restrain him from behind. The marshal gained purchase around David's torso, pinning his arms. Then he began to drag him backward like a bag of horse feed.

Carvey had gone to O'Brien's aid while Kev Holt joined the mutually indecisive Barker on the tenuous ground between their wounded boss and his unwillingly retreating opponent. With Carvey and Beatrice bracing his rise from the floor, O'Brien glanced about with dazed eyes for his intended victim. Spotting him at last in Neill's control, he broke away from his wife's clinging embrace. Meantime Carvey and Barker both turned toward David and drew their guns. But O'Brien called this his fight and charged David with the fury of an incensed grizzly. A catastrophic impact was but seconds away. A panicked Marshal Neill lost his footing and went over like a falling tree, bringing David down upon himself. Winded by the impact, Neill was unable to prevent O'Brien's sweeping David up by the neck and pushing him through the air like a hooked slab of beef in an abattoir.

David crashed onto the face of the automatic piano with a tremendous crescendo in low C, triggering the thing to start playing a familiar show tune as it rolled backward and struck the wall. In another second or two O'Brien might've snapped David's neck but Neill sprang onto his friend's back, reaching around his shoulders and pushing down his forearms with his own weight. This action allowed David to defend himself while O'Brien was left vulnerable. He smashed his fists down on O'Brien's shoulders, rendering the giant's arms momentarily useless at his sides. Then he swung his right fist into O'Brien's left eye socket. The force of the blow toppled O'Brien, whose terrible cry was appropriate to the fresh mangling of his face. Again Neill found himself winded by the collapse of another, and was thus unable to thwart O'Brien's next effort.

The mounted sentry who had remained positioned on Main Street opposite the Saloon saw the body of David Cohen crash through a stained-glass window, split the hitch rail in two, and drop into the mud a dead weight.

Bloodied, bruised, swollen, and still stunned, O'Brien swung about unsteadily to face his men. Except for Holt, who remained attentive, they all cast their eyes downward.

"The Lord will remember this, Klyde O'Brien," his wife scolded as she hurried to aid his victim.

O'Brien regarded Marshal Neill. With a look of disappointment in Klyde, he was rising to his feet, clutching his chest.

Beatrice stormed back inside, her stare blasting her husband. "You murdered that boy."

He showed Beatrice his palms. "It was him or me."

Marshal Neill stood with a downcast visage in front of the sharp blades of glass thrusting like teeth from the window.

He pursed his lips to stop them trembling. Gone was the boy who, since his father died, had been like a son to him, an only son; and with him went what remained of Neill's vigor. Now there was nothing ahead of him but time, and what seemed too much of it. Making a trivial association, he withdrew his pocket watch from his vest. It was still ticking but its face was shattered.

O'Brien's good eye shifted frantically in its socket. "He started it, that boy. Y'all saw how badly he wanted it. Even struck first!"

Bootfalls resounded from the steps outside. Then O'Brien's sentry lurched into the Saloon brandishing his rifle.

"Well what do you intend with *that?*" O'Brien mocked. "The boy came in, and he went out. Anybody see?"

"Doubt it, shops is shut up."

"Good. Drag 'im inside quick."

The sentry seemed to register his boss' broken features. Then he nodded and left.

Without a word, Marshal Neill turned and took his leave through the rear. As he brushed past Holt, their eyes met with the barest acknowledgment. Then Holt bent over the billiards table and intentionally sank the eight ball.

Chapter Eight

The kindling in Benjamin's fireplace still crackled and glowed and yet afforded the fleeting lovers small warmth as they spent their last moments together, but not entangled. In the quiet gloom of dawn, Sally, sitting up in bed with the covers bunched around her bosom, looked on as Benjamin, hunched over the desk where his gun sling lay flat, was applying wax to the channels of his two holsters for faster draws. At last he rose, and with accustomed agility fastened the belt to his hips, slipped his guns into place and tied them down. Next, he strapped on the shoulder holster.

In her growing melancholy Sally wondered why Benjamin bothered to pack if he was just minutes from getting himself killed. Without letting her brooding distract him, he crossed to the window and from a safe angle assessed the weather conditions. With a frown he dropped the curtain back into place and donned his wide-brimmed hat.

"I'll make a pot of coffee," she said.

Alone there, they went downstairs, Sally straight to the kitchen to fire up the kettle. As David got weekends off, he was far from her thoughts.

The dining hall was bathed in the now fiery light of sunrise. Benjamin rested his saddlebags on the floor and mounted a barstool, assuming a deceptively incautious position with his back to the door, which between two windows resembled a missing tooth in the mirror opposite him. When Sally went around to unbolt the inner gate he paid special attention to her reflected movements. Thus, when she swung the gate open he did not fail to notice the hands that immediately gripped the notched crests of the batwing doors from outside. He pivoted around in his chair, itching the handles of his sidearms.

Marshal James Neill parted the doors to reveal himself topped by his Stetson and wrapped in a buckskin coat split over his gun butt. With the doors flapping behind him, he dropped his hands to his sides, keeping his right hand a safe distance from his weapon. The two men exchanged a brief acknowledgment before Marshal Neill greeted Sally with his eyes. His face was pink from the cold.

"I smell coffee cooking," he said.

"Don't mind if you do," Sally replied with terse familiarity.

With the thumb and forefinger of his left hand, Marshal Neill reached cautiously across his waist to his holster. He slowly withdrew his weapon and dangled it in the air for her collection.

At this suspicious disarmament Benjamin made quick glances at all the potential firing points—windows, doors, dim corners.

Sally couldn't hide her astonishment. "That doesn't apply to you, Jim."

"I see it don't apply to him either. But take it. I insist."

"Out of respect for our marshal," Sally told Benjamin, "I should ask the same of you."

"Forget it," said Marshal Neill, stepping forward without removing his hat. "Let 'im keep his weapons. There's no sense his unpacking."

After hesitating, Sally accepted the marshal's gun and tucked it into her skirt.

To Benjamin, she said, "Don't make me use it."

Benjamin swung off the barstool.

Though Marshal Neill was about a head shorter than him, his compact and sinewy form held its own menace. If he was intimidated by the bigger man's stature he didn't show it. They stood face to face, gazes locked in silence.

"How 'bout that coffee?" Sally gave them her backside and hurriedly went into the kitchen, returning with equal urgency holding a steaming kettle.

The marshal forced a smile and extended his hand. "Hello, Ben," he said.

But Benjamin merely gritted his teeth and clenched his fists.

His gesture ignored, Marshal Neill motioned toward the bar counter, where Sally was pouring their cups full. He took a seat, leaving Benjamin standing awkwardly behind him.

Immediately Neill began warming his hands around his cup.

To his back, Benjamin said, "You disarmed as if you were entering a church. So, confess."

Neill responded at his reflection in the cup. "I mean to reconcile with you, Ben. Privately."

Opposite him, Sally protested. "I'm not going anywhere, Jim."

The marshal shook his head. "Ain't fit for a woman's ears, Sally."

"I ain't leaving you two alone," she replied, "so start your talking."

Now came the pitter-patter of fresh drizzle on the entrance overhang.

Neill's eyes remained remote in the shadows beneath his lowered brow. Suddenly he lifted them toward Sally. "Well then, let's get right down to it," he began with a sigh. "Long time back, Ben lost his woman."

At this Sally couldn't help feeling a pang of jealousy, but it was hardly the moment for such emotions. She stifled it. "Had to be something like that," she reacted.

"Murdered," Benjamin muttered.

Neill twisted around, chin raised. "But Ben doesn't know for sure who did it, and why."

For his part, Benjamin remained remote. Sally could sense his pent breath.

"Would you sit and talk to me, Ben?" Neill asked.

His caring shocked Sally. More than just history, these men seemed to share a kind of respect, maybe even more.

"You've come a long way for justice," he continued. "I understand that. But you want the truth, too, so hear me out. Come and sit down."

For Benjamin to do as the marshal told must have taken a lot, but—possibly because he was under Sally's scrutiny—he grudgingly took a seat two barstools up, keeping one foot on the floor.

Neill thanked him for it. This small victory won, the marshal felt sufficiently comfortable to take his first sip of coffee—and thus so did a relieved Sally. In a constricted voice he continued, "There's something else. Something you don't expect, Ben. Let's start with that."

They witnessed Benjamin brace himself with a breath that expanded his chest and broadened his shoulders in his slicker.

"She was pregnant," said Neill.

Sally gasped. "My God...."

Benjamin's unforgiving countenance seemed to collapse in on itself, and his eyes began darting in confusion. Finally, he spoke. "But she told *you?*"

"She hoped it would get you two your freedom."

Still in disbelief, Benjamin allowed himself to dodge the obvious implications of Neill's story. But suddenly his big head slumped forward. Then, collecting himself, he rolled up his chin and stepped off his chair. The look in his eyes revealed a mixed torment.

Sally saw the situation unravelling. She gripped the gun butt protruding from her waistband.

"Easy Sally," Neill told her. "I'll continue. That is, if you'll let me, Ben."

Again, here was a convivial usage of Benjamin's first name, its warmer-sounding diminutive to be exact. This worked on Benjamin. He stepped back onto his seat.

Addressing Sally, the marshal continued. "Back in '61, Ben here worked on my family's plantation in Virginia. Neill *King* Cotton we called it. Klyde was our overseer."

Benjamin interrupted, sharply. "I did not work for your family. I *belonged* to it. As did my father and his father. And Klyde O'Brien was slave master."

Neill swallowed, nodded. "Fair enough. I reckon to this day Ben wears the scars of a lashing that might've killed him. His woman begged me to intervene with Klyde, and I set my price."

Sally stiffened. "You what?"

"Don't rub it in, Sally. Think I'm proud of it?"

Again Benjamin's gaze plunged, the brim of his hat masking his mournful expression. The sound of rainfall swelled into a roar.

"Klyde killed her," Sally concluded. "He found out she was with child, a child that might've been yours, James Neill!"

Marshal Neill breathed out before betraying his friend, the color leaving his face, the light dimming behind his eyes. "I wasn't aware of his plan. That's the God's truth. The war had just begun, and I thought maybe I could get 'em both on a blockade runner bound for Cuba. Next thing I knew she was killed."

"And then you ran like rabbits," said Sally.

Neill's square shoulders collapsed in his buckskin jacket. "Not for that, Sally. I saw no cause to hang around waiting to be conscripted or killed in a slave revolt. I was just a kid. Our intention was to return after the war. But by '65 there wasn't much to return to."

"I managed my own escape soon afterward," Benjamin offered, finally. "I put a sickle in the eye of your cousin, Jeb, to clear my path."

"You did him a favor," Neill responded. "He didn't serve. He's got ten grandkids and my old property."

Benjamin suddenly reached for the lapel of his slicker, causing the marshal to flinch. But rather than digging inside, he merely bent it back. Revealed was *his* star—the bronze Medal of Honor and its bas-relief of Minerva, the Roman goddess of warriors, repulsing a snake-wielding representation of Discord.

Marshal Neill gave it some respectful attention. "I heard all about you in Cheyenne—from a young fellow who worked for Attorney General Knox. They sure got a history on you."

"They ought to," Benjamin replied, releasing his lapel. "The Department of Justice and I go way back."

Marshal Neill changed the subject. "Ben, you won't leave here alive without my help. What good is it getting shot up and lynched by Klyde's boys?"

Benjamin replied, "Sometimes freedom is worth dying for."

"That's stupid. You can pick wiser fights. And live for more of 'em."

The so-called prophet leaned forward. "Marshal, I didn't come here to talk." He got to his feet and looked down, way down, at Neill.

A faint voice now called through the storm. It was O'Brien's. "Come on out, blacky! I got some news for you! Come on out! I'm the man you want!"

Neill stood up, revealing nothing more. "You've busted enough rocks, Ben," he entreated. "Time to lay down that hammer of yours and rest. Let me take you into custody. We can be on the next train to Cheyenne. You won't spend more than a week in jail."

"An offer I can refuse."

Without disengaging from Benjamin, Neill held out his hand to Sally. "My weapon?"

With some reluctance, she handed it over.

Neill weighed it in his grasp and shifted his view to Benjamin. The men shared a long, measured moment. Finally, the marshal's eyes wavered and he holstered the revolver. He dismissed Benjamin with a curt nod, and, turning his back on him again, sat down at the bar before his coffee cup. Over his shoulder, Sally gave Benjamin a worried—last?—look.

To Neill's back, Benjamin said, "Don't interfere." With spurs ringing he walked out into the rain.

* * *

Poised in the center of Main Street, at a remove of about twenty paces, Klyde O'Brien gripped his buffalo rifle sideways at his waist. A stream of rainwater fell from the tip of his hat between his eyes, one swollen shut, the other following his opponent as Benjamin stepped down into the mud and revealed his short guns with a parting of his jacket. Meantime, a few paces behind O'Brien's left shoulder, the old war veteran Jesse Larcan leaned against the driving rain, wielding a shotgun. As for O'Brien's other helpers, they were all suspiciously absent—likely positioned, Benjamin guessed, on rooftops or between storefronts to back-shoot him when he drew. Visible behind Larcan was the shattered stained-glass window of the Saloon, a curiosity Benjamin registered but couldn't dwell on. He stopped his cautious advance in the middle of Main Street, working his fingers to maintain nimbleness. Sheets of rain lashed the back of his slicker and the wind whistled in his ears. To avoid blinking, he squinted at O'Brien and at the same time found his balance on the uneven ground by keeping his knees unlocked and leaning into the arches of his feet. His breathing was just as deliberate—unhurried, readying drags.

"Jimmy promised to help her was all!" O'Brien yelled. "I did the rest." His swollen lips grinned. "I laid her flat and brung the axe down."

Enraged though Benjamin was, he wouldn't be provoked—at least not yet—into a first draw.

O'Brien chuckled through the rain. "What's more, your little Jew helper stirred up some trouble at the Saloon last night."

Suddenly the significance of Klyde's rearranged face—and David's absence from the scene—became evident. Benjamin filled his lungs.

"Yep. Nasty what he done to me, Ben."

Klyde began to step steadily through the mist with Larcan following. "Gave me a damn proper beating for my sins," he added.

Now, for Benjamin, the broken glass yonder registered with more import.

A sudden rifle cock to his side ended Benjamin's temptation to reach for his guns. But unable to shift his focus from O'Brien, he couldn't see Sally hefting his Winchester on her porch. One feeling of alarm melded into another when he heard her cry, "What've you done to him, Klyde?"

Just then Marshal Neill burst outside through the swinging doors and, pushing the rifle down, grappled with Sally for it. When he ripped it from her grasp she slapped him so hard across the jaw he nearly lost his footing. But he quickly recovered his senses and stuck a finger in her face.

"Don't test me!" he threatened.

Undeterred, she replied. "Don't be a fool."

While O'Brien had carelessly watched this drama play out, confident in his hidden guns, Benjamin's eyes never strayed from his target.

It was time.

O'Brien's face strained into another gruesome smile. "I killed 'im, nigger. I tossed the Jew bastard through my window. He expired face down in horse shit."

Benjamin sprang to the side, his hands flicking to draw. But, while Klyde reacted not at all, from behind Benjamin came the distinct sounds of misfires.

Having failed to induce O'Brien to draw first, Benjamin saw his opponent's flushed pallor blanch, and he was about to learn why.

The voice of Kev Holt called out, "Carvey, Barker, toss those guns aside!"

Down Main Street—and visible to Sally and Neill only by sharp turns of their chins—Holt was shoving his gun barrel into the back of Slim Barker's neck while grabbing Jack Carvey by the scruff of the collar.

O'Brien roared: "Hell you doing, Kev?"

The gaunt figure answered, "These men are nailed for attempted murder."

"What!"

For his part, Marshal Neill seemed confounded. But as Holt gave his reply he lowered his head in realization—and complete capitulation.

"Thus far you're only a conspirator, O'Brien," Holt called. "Ain't that right, Marshal? And there's a fair argument to be made that you killed the boy in self-defense. But if you gun down Benjamin Neill, I'll make sure you hang."

"Reveal yourself, Judas!" O'Brien cried.

Neill had guessed right. "A detective, Klyde," he said. "Assigned by Washington to follow Ben."

Now the trembling figures of Carvey and Barker dropped their guns into the mud.

Holt promptly shoved them in Neill's direction, thereby removing himself from the line of fire.

Klyde O'Brien pivoted toward Neill. "Help me, Jim…."

Marshal Neill shook his head. "Let it go, Klyde. He's going to put everything that's happened here into a report. And I gotta do the same."

Resting the Winchester's barrel on his shoulder, Neill turned his back on his old friend and left Sally alone on the porch, the doors flapping.

O'Brien swung around to Larcan. After his old friend nodded, Klyde spun his enormous frame back to Benjamin.

But Benjamin merely smiled.

"Draw!" Klyde cried, "*Draw!*"

But Benjamin's smile merely broadened.

"Slap leather, damnit! *Draw! Draw!*"

O'Brien gasped for breath, his complexion dappled with purple. His chest heaved.

Benjamin had him. He twitched his fingers enough to force O'Brien into the draw he demanded.

Larcan, too, began to raise his weapon.

* * *

A spot appeared on Klyde O'Brien's forehead and Benjamin's bullet led his brains out behind. His second shot struck Larcan in the chest and he too fell flat on his back, dead.

Benjamin holstered his Colts, thrust his hands into the pockets of his slicker, and swung himself around to face

Carvey and Barker, under Holt's guard at the hitch post of the S&S. He glided forward with a scowl. Shrieking, the men dropped to their knees in unison. One after another, they received the point of his boot in their faces, falling backward into the muck.

Wind and rain whipped violently about Benjamin as he watched the sobbing men attempting to squirm away in separate directions.

Holt showed his badge to Benjamin. "Pinkerton Detective Agency, Denver," he said.

Benjamin looked up from the panicked bodies. "I should've guessed yesterday."

"I was told you might."

"Who sent you out? The *good* Pinkerton?"

Holt nodded. "If you mean Ferdinand Schavers, yes. The man who stood at Mr. Lincoln's side with Allan Pinkerton himself. He told me you stood at Grant's."

Benjamin avoided reminiscing. "For his sake, I haven't spoken with Ferdinand in years. How'd he know?"

"Paul Dunbar at *The Denver Post*. You revealed your plans to him last week. Your friends didn't accept them as a farewell. To top it off, the day after you rode outta Denver a letter arrived by special delivery from the British trade office. You've been invited on a speaking tour of England. According to Schavers, Dunbar's attorney is appealing again for the restoration of your right to travel."

"I see," said Benjamin. "Ferdy sent you here to tell me that, but you joined O'Brien instead."

Holt shook his head, then nodded toward the corpses. "I'm more than an errand boy. I reckoned we could kill two birds with one stone."

"And what if O'Brien had killed me a minute ago?"

"He had little chance against you. That was obvious from the start." Holt motioned to Carvey and Barker, still clawing the mud, whimpering. "Anyway, David returned our sidearms loaded with dummy bullets. So, even if I hadn't been here to look after you...."

Benjamin stepped up onto the covered porch where Sally was waiting. "You protected the wrong man. David would have been more worthy of your efforts."

"I was on the wrong side of the action last night," Holt confessed. "The marshal intervened. But there was no stopping that boy. He picked a fight he couldn't win."

Benjamin fixed him, severely. "What's your full name?"

Kev Holt told him. "Brought my horse up on the Union Pacific to Hillsdale and arrived before you did. Figured the best way to acquaint with the situation was from O'Brien's camp."

Presently Marshal Neill, fortified with Sally's whiskey, stepped out onto the porch. Initially he surveyed Main Street, a mournful look in his eyes. Soaking in bloody, rain-washed pools, O'Brien and Larcan's corpses were attracting the emergent townspeople like flies to shit. Preacher O'Conner, having crawled out of his sanctuary at the Mercantile, was already saying prayers over them.

"As a federal agent," Neill told Holt, "it was incumbent on you to identify yourself upon my return from Cheyenne."

Holt would not be intimidated. "You wanna lose that star of yours?"

In response, Marshal Neill's voice dropped to a rasp. "Spur your horse hard, detective. Before the coffin maker gets a corpse richer." Then, to Benjamin, he added:

"What to say, Ben? I hope the future will be kinder to you."

With that, he got Carvey and Barker on their feet for transfer to jail and marched them ahead of himself through the gathering crowd in Main Street.

* * *

Sally bolted the iron door behind herself and Benjamin. Through it they could still hear the commotion from outside, particularly the cries of Beatrice O'Brien who cursed the marshal between sobs. Benjamin removed his hat and eased onto a barstool while Sally went behind the counter. She poured them each a drink from the bottle Marshal Neill had left standing on the bar.

Benjamin bowed his head. Droplets fell from the tip of his nose to the wood counter. He asked Sally for a pencil and paper. She maneuvered around the bar and sat next to him. On a small notepad he drew the six-pointed Star of David. "It should appear on his stone," he told her. Over his shoulder he saw her cheeks lined with tears. He smudged some away with his thumb.

"A fine young man," she said. "He watches us now from his home on high."

Replied Benjamin with a hint of song, *"Between earth and sky, thought I heard my savior cry...."*

Sally took a sip of whiskey while he pushed his glass around on the counter, near his rifle. After a moment, she added, "Only two people are mourning out there, Klyde's widow and David's girl. The rest are considering their advantage."

"And you? You've probably lost more than a few customers."

"There's only two watering holes in town. The one whose future is now in doubt isn't this one. What's your next step?"

"I hadn't planned one, frankly." He took a drink, coughed. "Except perhaps to ride out of here. I think I'll disappear into the mountains for a while. Passing a few weeks in a peaceful pine forest sounds mighty fine." He got to his feet.

"What do I owe you, Sally?"

"Take good care of yourself, Ben."

She grasped his hands. They shared a moment.

Then Benjamin pulled away and gathered up his bags, awkwardly embracing them with one arm. With his free hand he accepted his long gun from Sally.

"I'll show you to the stables," she said.

"I know my way."

He bent over to kiss her cheek and she pressed her face firmly to his lips.

Outside the storm had finally abated and the muddy ground now glistened in shafts of sunlight poking through the clouds. For the first time in days a temperate breeze greeted Benjamin's skin as he stepped into the subdued light of day. Alone he crossed to the stables and set down his bags on the bed of scattered hay inside the door. Against the doorframe he leaned his rifle. The old stallion beyond seemed to recognize his master's scent, snorting and whinnying from his cell. But before responding to these overtures Benjamin stepped into David's forlorn office for a parting look around.

He noticed two books on the desk.

Atop the familiar Old Testament was the similarly tattered copy of Shakespeare's *Othello*.

Among other volumes, David had received it from him nights ago. Benjamin approached the desk and retrieved *Othello* with care, running his fingers over its coarse blue knit cover and weighing the slim volume in his hands as if it were made of gold. Instead of tucking the tragedy into one of his saddlebags he flipped to its last act. Finding the passage he sought almost at once, he circled it with David's pencil and left its pages open on the desk for Sally to spot. The scripture he shoved into a jacket pocket.

Next, he went to release his horse, whose graying head bobbed impatiently over the transom. Benjamin unbolted and swung open the gate while accepting an affectionate brush of the animal's cushioned muzzle against his cheek and a rude snort in his ear.

He led his friend up the hay-littered corridor to the tack room. The stallion stamped and neighed and shook his mane as Benjamin rigged him for travel and patted his rump and talked soothingly to him. Finally, Benjamin guided him outdoors where he slipped boot into stirrup and mounted up with a peal of leather and a groan of fatigue. Then, after throwing a conclusive glance toward the backside of the Sun and Sagebrush Inn, he reined his partner west onto a path that ran behind the buildings facing Main Street. Thus rider and horse quietly departed, and as they did they were caught in a teary gaze from a second floor window.

For the first time, Jeannie McIntyre laid eyes on this Negro stranger whose influence had abruptly relieved her of the burden of an impossible love, a girlish and naive love, she now realized.

Far from hating him for it, she discovered she didn't even bear him a grudge; she just let Benjamin ride on without uttering an unkind word in his tracks.

That afternoon Sally found the copy of *Othello* lying open on the desk in the stables. She hungrily read the passage Benjamin had left for her to discover; but it was only later, when Marshal Neill revealed what he'd learned in Cheyenne, that she would grasp its full significance:

> *I have done the state some service, and they know't.*
> *No more of that. I pray you, in your letters,*
> *When you shall these unlucky deeds relate,*
> *Speak of me as I am, nothing extenuate*
> *Nor set down aught in malice.*

Epilogue

When Kev Holt stepped off the train from Laramie people took notice. Except for an occasional visit by mining brass, or when the Chinese, Irish, Welsh, and black miners descended in eager hoards upon the whorehouse and saloon, the town of Louise saw few strangers.

At the waist of his knee-length canvas slicker he held his horse's saddle, blanket, and bit. From his right shoulder hung his saddlebags. He squinted against the curtains of dust thrown up by passing lorries. What was registered with the state Land Office as a municipality consisted merely of a mercantile and a boarding house, a stable and a church, and a few more structures, each identifiable by its painted sign—the unadorned *Church* otherwise indistinguishable from the nondescript *Saloon*—and all of them erected by the town's corporate patrons whose trustees occupied its highest offices.

Beyond the single line of crude buildings rose steep foothills zigzagged by a switchback trail leading to the town's mainstay, the iron ore mines dug into "the Winds"—the Wind River Range.

Over these distant peaks the autumn sky was blackening with thunderheads. Holt had little time.

Those locals who held Holt suspiciously in their sights watched him move confidently to the livestock car aft. At the top of the planked loading ramp he fitted his roan with her bridle before leading her down; below, as he fixed the girth, he noticed a U.S. Postal Service courier two cars back wheeling out stuffed mail bags. From the boxcar between himself and the courier, miners both white and black rolled heavy equipment, aided by draft animals. As Holt led his horse around them he elicited a few furtive glances—that is, until he flashed the courier with something in the palm of his hand. This made all stop and stare.

Was it a bribe or a badge?

"Thirsty?" Holt asked him.

The barrel-bellied man cracked a smile. "Information for the price of a drink?"

"I'll make it a double."

The man looked him over, licking sweat from his upper lip. He nodded.

Holt led his horse to the saloon and tied her to the hitch rail alongside another mare. Nailed to the door was a sign:

NOTICE:
EXPECTORATION AND PISSING
IN AND AROUND THE PREMISES ARE
PROHIBITED BY LAW.
ANY PERSON GUILTY OF VIOLATING THE SAME
WILL BE PROSECUTED.

The saloon had but one dusty window. When Holt swung open the rough, unfinished door it threw a shaft of light onto some empty tables and a bar resembling a pine coffin box. Two men were leaning against the bar counter, a dark bottle between them. Chewing their cigars, they appraised him from behind a cloud of smoke. He shut the door and paused to let his eyes adjust while his nostrils twitched at the wretched mix of odors—smoke, sweat, and greasy cooking. Then he approached the counter where a bearded barman leaned toward him with both hands flat down and his dirty sleeves rolled up.

"Two whiskeys," said Holt.

The barman put two glasses on the counter and poured the first round. "Ten cents a pour. Seventy-five for the half-bottle."

"Leave it there," Holt responded. Then, "Why was such a sooty town as this given the pretty name?"

The barman, asquint, scrutinized Holt and his tailored attire before answering. "Why don't you address that question to the chairman of the mining company?"

"I see. Mistress or mother-in-law?"

His sarcasm countered, the barman reacted with an amused grin.

The saloon door opened with a pop, causing Holt to wheel around and draw his six-gun. But it was only the courier. He holstered his firearm and turned back to the bar. The locals were now giving him twice the eye as before but the courier quickly filled the gap between them and Holt. He downed his drink and studied Holt over his shoulder. "Well? What's on your mind, Mr. Quick Draw?"

Holt clawed his new Vandyke beard with a touch of embarrassment. "I'm searching for a man."

"No surprise in that." He gestured toward Holt's gun. "What man and why?"

"*Why* ain't important," replied Holt. Then he told him *what* man.

The courier nodded. "Comes this way once or twice a year. Talks to the miners—you know, speechifies. Sings pretty good too. Friendly with some folks up the west forest road."

"Folks?"

"Colored folks," said the courier. "Run a small mercantile and postal station halfway to the mines. He gives his sermons from its steps. Can't say he's popular with the mining company. They hire you?"

Holt swallowed his drink and shook his head. He poured them a second round. "I reckon I just follow the switchback?"

The courier nodded and threw back his whiskey. "'Bout half a day's ride from here. I'm heading that way myself with a shipment of goods. But first there's the mail from Laramie to sort. I don't set out till tomorrow."

"I can't wait," said Holt.

"Course you can't." The courier examined him again. So did the barman. And so did the two locals. Holt slapped some coins on the counter. He emptied his glass and pulled on his riding gloves. As he stepped away the courier asked, "Just what has ol' Ben done?"

"He's done—and said—some things," was the reply. "Good or bad depends who's judging." Holt tipped his hat and left.

The courier turned to the barman. "That man ain't coming back."

Indeed, he would not.

* * *

The wind was blowing hard when Holt reached the outpost, the scent of spruce and hemlock pine strong in the wind, the ground sprinkled with crisp brown needles. Obscured in an ever cloudier sky the sun hung somewhere not far above the wall of mountains. By the damp, drafty air Holt reckoned showers were imminent. He tied his horse and made his entrance. His spurs ringing with each step, the brittle panels creaked under his boots. The interior was wanting in stocks. There was a faint scent of wood smoke from the proprietor's lodgings in back.

"What can we do for you?" The voice was guarded.

Behind the counter stood a well-built black man in a flannel shirt and braces, a woman beside him. Their teenaged son was cleaning a breech loading rifle at a table to Holt's right.

Holt stepped forward.

"I'm looking for a colored man."

"Well, you found two," answered the youth. "And two's better than one."

The boy might be trouble, thought Holt. He unfastened the top buttons of his slicker and reached inside. The youth slid a slug into the relic rifle.

Before withdrawing his hand, Holt said, "If I intended to reach for my weapon my jacket would be open at the waist."

"Let 'im alone," the man told his son.

Holt withdrew a badge. "Kev Holt. Pinkerton Detective Agency, Denver. I'm trying to locate Benjamin Neill."

"Don't know him."

The reply came quick, too quick.

"I got something for him," he said. "It's my duty to deliver it."

"I *said*, I don't know him."

Again Holt reached inside his slicker. He sensed the boy ready with the rifle as he extended a sealed envelope to his father. But nobody moved. "This subpoena," Holt continued, "orders Benjamin Neill to Washington D.C. for a hearing at the State Department. His friends are trying to restore his right to travel."

"And you?"

"I'm doing my part too."

The man's resolve wavered. With a sideways glance he deferred to his wife for approval.

"He can't read," said the boy of his father. "Give it here." Leaving the rifle on the table he stood up and snatched the envelope from Holt, who watched impatiently as he ripped it open and flipped through the pages.

As Holt accepted the papers back the rafters above wheezed from a sudden gust. The woman finally spoke and the stranger knew a decision had been made.

"If he don't expect you, he'll kill you," she said.

Holt shook his head. "He knows me. It's the second time I've borne him good news. Maybe now he'll be willing to listen."

"Listening is the easy part," she said. "It's keeping his mouth shut that's difficult." She pointed to the door. "Spot the highest peak northwest. Head for it and you'll find your way onto the trail. It's a steep ride but after about an hour you'll leave the forest and find his cabin."

"I thank you, ma'am." Holt tipped his hat and left.

She turned to her husband. "Let's hope this time he lets his lawyer do the talking."

* * *

The jagged snow-capped peaks shown pale blue in the early evening light. Beneath the talus slopes the lodgepole cabin looked bold and defiant. Smoke rose from the chimney. A light rain was falling, and the brim of Holt's Stetson afforded him scant protection from it. Sitting on his mount with water dripping from his chin he espied the cabin from the shelter of the treeline below. His mare stamped her hooves, desirous of the two-horse shed beside the cabin where another horse was sheltered. "You're gonna get it," Holt told her. They started up the hill and past the last of the pines, deformed and bare from almost total exposure to the elements. At this altitude autumn conditions lasted only a month; the snow remained into June.

Alarmed neighs issued from the stable. A stallion's dark head nodded over the transom. Holt dismounted and let fall the reins. He approached the cabin door. The structure was old but strong. In that terrain it had to be strong to be old. Abandoned long ago by its owner it was open to anybody needing shelter. If there were dishes inside, they would be washed by one traveler and left clean for the next. But the cabin's accommodations had already been claimed by somebody else.

Holt rapped on the door. Nothing. He knocked again. "Neill, open up!"

No response.

"Neill, I say, open up!"

He unfastened the lower buttons of his slicker as a precaution. Then he pulled the right wing over the grip of his .44. The door was cumbersome. It groaned open.

"Neill!" he called again, stepping inside.

To his left was the south wall of the cabin and what sufficed as a kitchen. In the space before him were a table and two chairs. On the right was a lighted fireplace and near it a door, presumably to a bedroom or storeroom. Little else was visible.

Holt turned to check behind the door.

Just then, it was thrust violently against his right shoulder, spinning his body like an axle pin. With his arm weakened by the blow he failed to raise his gun fast enough to defend himself. His opponent handily knocked the gun away and pushed him backward over the table. The momentum caused Holt to tumble to the floor. Automatically, he sprang to his feet—only to receive the end of the table in his groin, pinning him to the wall behind. The flickering firelight danced along the imposing outline of his aggressor, opposite, as he drew a revolver from his hip encasement.

In the ensuing pause each man shared recognition.

"Well!" said Benjamin Neill, slipping his sidearm into its carbine boot. "*Kev Holt* from the Pinkertons of Denver—now with whiskers and a new suit of clothes."

Holt grimaced, his body still stuck between table and wall. "Benjamin Neill," he muttered. "Same as before."

"You know," said Benjamin, "it's unwise to unbutton your coat at the waist. Unless of course you're the faster draw."

Holt winced. "Unpin me, Neill. You nailed my hip."

"I beg your pardon. That's the first place I looked, and I saw it adorned." He pulled the table away from Holt. "I'll start a lamp," he said.

Now free, Holt rubbed his side and scanned the floor for his gun. Benjamin kicked it across to him. He put a kerosene lamp on the table and set it aglow with a match. A blue shirt was revealed hugging his broad torso, tucked into grey dungarees secured with a thick cowhide belt. In back of him, his Winchester rifle leaned against the doorjamb.

Holt holstered his gun. "I wish to stable my horse if you don't mind."

"By all means, stay the night. Canned meat and potatoes for dinner. As for your horse, you'll find plenty of feed in there and a dry blanket. Meantime I'll put some coffee on."

When Holt returned, the oak table was set for dinner and the coffee was steaming on the stovetop. He took the seat facing the kitchen. Benjamin brought over the kettle and poured their tin cups full. He remained standing to attend to dinner.

"Hot coffee at the end of the trail," said Holt. "I'm obliged."

Benjamin nodded over the rim of his cup.

Holt sipped his coffee.

"My dear friend Ferdy Schavers sent you?" Benjamin asked.

"Same as last time. Dunbar at the *Post* contacted our office. You're easy to track. People remember you."

"That they remember me to you is another matter."

Holt's brow creased. "Your friends downhill did good for you. Forget it. Last summer, I reported that Dunbar's attorney was appealing again for the issuance of your passport. But instead of returning with me to Denver you stole out the back way. After all your friends in Denver tried to do for you, and after David gave up his life for you, I had to ride back alone. I felt bad about that."

Benjamin put down his cup. "Me too. But I couldn't bear to linger there, even for another hour. David was sure the marshal would protect him like a son."

"He protected him more like a nephew. He could've done more, he could've drawn his gun against O'Brien. Had he, there would've been no killing at all."

Benjamin set a pair of tins on the grill, one marked *Pot Roast,* the other *Taters.*

Holt nodded toward the stove. "So this is what David's sacrifice has enabled? You might be satisfied ending your days eating canned food in seclusion, but a writer in England is offering you a more worthy future. He's founded the *Let Benjamin Neill Travel Society,* sponsored by a group called the Fabians—I'm told you know the organization."

"We go back. A travel society? Really?"

"What's more," Holt continued, "twenty-seven members of Parliament have signed a letter inviting you on a 'singing' tour of England. I presume that's code for 'speaking.' The State Department has agreed to another hearing."

He withdrew the subpoena along with the letter from Paul Lawrence Dunbar, the black poet and journalist.

Benjamin received them and gave the subpoena a cursory glance. He shook the papers at Holt. "Signed by a proven oppressor who calls himself Secretary of State!" But Dunbar's letter elicited a much closer reading. Another name jumped out at him—that of his would-be British host, George Bernard Shaw.

"Things've changed, Neill."

Benjamin folded the papers carefully and tucked them into his shirt pocket. Then he served up dinner.

Holt dug in. "You're quite a cook," he quipped between chews.

Benjamin merely stared down at his own plate. "Things *have* changed," he conceded.

Suddenly he convulsed in a fit of coughing that shook the table and bloodstained his eyes. Half a minute passed before it ran its course.

Holt swallowed with effort. "Your health's no better, I see."

After a long, restorative breath, Benjamin said, "Now perhaps you understand the urgency of my previous ride and my reluctance today to embark on a new journey."

"Winter's coming, Neill. You won't make it."

"My destiny's fulfilled," he sighed. He took a reluctant bite of his food. "I saw myself staying on here."

Holt patted the corners of his mouth with a cloth napkin and leaned forward. "I've come to take you back. Schavers tells me there's real hope for you this time. He insists you go to Washington. Dunbar's lawyer will accompany you. Haven't you often said you gotta keep fighting?"

Benjamin pushed his food around on his plate. Then, looking up, he answered, "Until I'm dying."

"Take that boot out of your coffin," said Holt, "and saddle up."

* * *

The sky awakened from its stormy slumber a solid blue. To the west, the granite and shale slopes of the Winds loomed ivory in the dawn light. Burdened with their saddlebags, Benjamin and Holt left the cabin one after the other, lowering their chins against the explosion of sunlight. Slapping the leather on their horses, the men released them to limber up for the journey. Benjamin's mix of Arabian and quarter horse, grey around the muzzle and belly, still commanded attention from man and beast alike. Holt's mare followed him this way and that like an obedient colt. For a short time the men took pleasure in watching their horses getting acquainted thus. Then they rigged and claimed their mounts. Holt automatically drew his horse east toward Louise.

"No. This way!" Benjamin reined his stallion south.

Holt protested. In that direction, it was an overnight ride to the Union Pacific.

"It's stunning this time of year," replied Benjamin. "Come along."

Shaking his head, Holt reined his animal to follow.

For hours they cut downhill through an evergreen forest glistening from light shattered by a gentle pine needle cover. A sharp northerly wind wafted through the trees with a sound suggestive of a rolling creek ahead, always ahead. As the ground leveled, brightness glowed beyond. They soon rode into a wide red rock valley with a base of sweeping yellow grass and burgundy sage bushes and walls of maroon scrub oak and golden aspen aglitter. They drew rein, one after the other, sharing an awestruck appreciation of their surroundings. Beyond this autumn-spangled valley lay a vast ashen prairie and the railway to Denver.

"Let's ride," said Benjamin.

Acknowledgments

Any Man's Land by Alexander Helwig Wyant, c. 1880,
courtesy of the Los Angeles County Museum of Art.

All Man's Land was first completed back in 1990 as an independent study project under the guidance of Prof. William H. Brown of the University of Southern California's Department of English. Bill was a generous mentor whose penchant for quoting Chaucer found its way into the book. The late Edward V. "Mike" Foreman of Minneapolis—music scholar, author, and voice coach—contributed significantly to my knowledge of Paul Robeson and my appreciation of his musical gifts. Mike was a dear family friend and I miss his warmth, his wit, and his brilliance. Writer and former co-editor of *The Prague Revue,* David Speranza, copyedited the manuscript for publication.

The title was inspired by Alexander Helwig Wyant's *Any Man's Land* (above), a painting whose quiet beauty arrested my attention on a visit to LACMA in 1988 and whose title got me thinking.

Fortuitously, my work on *All Man's Land* coincided with the publication of Martin Duberman's landmark biography *Paul Robeson.* I wasn't the first in my family to read it. Just as I owed my discovery of Robeson's music to my grandparents, Lea and László Weiss, my copy of his biography came from Grandma Lea too. She had read Duberman's 900-page tome with devotion—and a dictionary at her side. What struck her most, I recall, was the sense of dignity instilled in Robeson by his parents—his father an escaped slave who earned a degree in theology and became a clergyman, and his mother, born in Pennsylvania, a schoolteacher. I remember Grandma Lea recounting in her Russian accent, "He was called a name in school, and his mother told him the boys were *jealous* of him because he had color and they *did not!*"

Further research brought me to the Wyoming State Capitol building and to Denver's Public Library of the West. An article in *Smithsonian Magazine* led me to the Black American West Museum in Denver's Five Points neighborhood. Its founder, the late Paul W. Stewart, was nothing short of inspiring as I dedicated myself to getting the historical details right.

Notes

That said, I took my share of liberties in the text. A few examples follow:

The Congressional Medal of Honor earned by Benjamin Neill was, in actual fact, awarded to African-American Private Thomas Hawkins whose bravery merits acknowledgment here. Although the 9th Cavalry had been deployed to Wyoming to settle a land war a decade before the events of *All Man's Land*, the troop was not present in the state in 1904. The African-American town of Deerfield, CO, wasn't established until 1910. Finally, the text's "Suspicious" Activities Control Act of 1889 anticipates the factual Subversive Activities Control Act of 1950. And so on.

Regarding Robeson's incendiary 1949 Paris Peace Conference statement to which the Introduction refers, some have proposed he was misquoted. According to the Associated Press, he said "It is unthinkable that American Negroes would go to war on behalf of those who have oppressed us for generations against the Soviet Union which in one generation has raised our people to full human dignity." Duberman, relying on a French transcript, offers a more nuanced statement while acknowledging that Robeson did, indisputably, make such a comment days later in Stockholm. In 1971, Paul Robeson Jr. read the very same AP quote to the Canadian Broadcasting Company (but with "could" for "would"). Later, he seems to have had second thoughts about its authenticity. Whatever the truth, the fateful Paris statement reported by the AP uses turns of phrase and content common to Robeson's speeches that curiously do not appear in the French transcript.

The novel includes several authentic historical references, including posted signs, postcard titles, and an excerpt from a U.S. State Department opinion on Robeson's demand for the renewal of his passport. A number of spirituals in Robeson's repertoire appear as well, all of them in the public domain.

Finally, Benjamin's Neill's weaponized use of the "Kaddish" by Rabbi Levi Yitzhak of Berditchev (1740-1809) is drawn from Robeson's own powerful use of this incantation in later years, and the form it appears in here is sourced from his version of it. In Benjamin Neill's voice it is intended to parallel Robeson's employment of his own signature song, "Ol' Man River," which evolved into a "battle cry" with a change of lyrics. For Robeson, *I'm tired of livin' and scared of dyin'* didn't have quite the punch of:

I must keep fighting until I'm dying!

About the Author

Born in Minneapolis in 1968, D. László Conhaim is the author, most recently, of *Comanche Captive* (Gale/Cengage, 2017), about a former Indian captive's struggle to reunite with her Comanche-born son. The sequel will be published in 2021. His first professional writing credit was a two-part 1986 interview in Los Angeles and Tokyo with Japanese screen legend Toshiro Mifune for Minneapolis' *City Pages*, followed by an interview with frequent costar Tatsuya Nakadai for USC's *Daily Trojan*. In 1995, Conhaim co-founded *The Prague Revue,* the longest-running literary journal to serve the community of international writers in Prague. For *TPR,* he wrote a fictional remembrance of Miguel de Unamuno, "Feeling into Don Miguel," which Gore Vidal "read with delight" and which Alexander Zaitchik (*Rolling Stone, The Nation*) called "masterful . . . a first-rate piece of writing by any standard" in *Think Magazine.* In 1999, TPR Books published his novel *Autumn Serenade,* a "mythomaniac's misadventure in Spain." He lives in Israel with his wife and two children.

Reading Group Primer:

An Interview with D. László Conhaim
By Michael Belfiore for *Us of America* magazine

Why, after the publication in 2017 of *Comanche Captive*, would you reach back nearly 30 years to publish a novella you wrote as a college student?

When *Comanche Captive* came out, I started receiving mail inquiring when I'd be publishing again. This followed ESPN's sports and culture website, *The Undefeated*, sadly omitting Paul Robeson from a long list of influential African Americans. It got me to thinking I should finally get *All Man's Land* out there—and in a way that called attention to Robeson.

After 30 years, surely you haven't published it as is.

I've thrown a fresh coat of paint on this one every five years or so, but I've always remained faithful to its original voice and structure. In preparing it for publication, I felt as if I was working as an editor to my younger self.

What inspired you to write *All Man's Land*?

The work that it came to be sort of fell under Robeson's spell. That story is told in the Introduction. I owe my admiration of him to my grandparents, who emigrated to the States from Eastern Europe where he was popular and where he found that his color wasn't a barrier.

Like Paul Robeson, your hero Benjamin Neill is a crusader for racial and social justice. But he is also a decorated Civil War hero. Is there any historical basis for such a character? And how specifically did you channel Robeson?

Benjamin Neill is a composite formed from several historical people, including one of 17 African Americans to receive the Congressional Medal of Honor for service in the Civil War. I should add that Robeson's own father served in the Union army, as did two of Frederick Douglass' sons. Robeson came along later than Douglass, of course, but set in 1904, *All Man's Land* takes place in his lifetime, and I found myself drawn principally to his story and to his spirit for inspiration.

Part of Benjamin Neill's backstory seems to closely resemble Robeson's fight against McCarthyism. But we also learn about a host of other figures apparently lost to history, including President Lincoln's first bodyguard, an African American.

I first learned about Ferdinand Schavers from Paul Stewart, the founder of Denver's Black American West Museum. It's astonishing that 30 years later nobody else seems to have written about him or put him on screen despite obvious opportunities to do so. There's so much yet to be told.

How did African Americans in the U.S. Army come to be called "buffalo soldiers"?

The commonly accepted explanation is that Native Americans compared the hair of the black troops serving in the Indian wars to that of the American bison. The image of a buffalo appeared on the 10th Cavalry's emblem until its deactivation in 1944.

All Man's Land follows *Comanche Captive* chronologically. Are there any through lines?

By 2021, when I publish *Comanche*'s sequel, *All Man's Land* will fall at the end of a trilogy chronologically. Though certainly not by any master plan, all of my American histories deal to some extent with the U.S. Cavalry's reliance on black regiments to do the dirty work of manifest destiny, including Indian removal.

I wanted to ask you about that. A conflict in the book emerges between Benjamin Neill and a black sergeant over that issue, and whether a black soldier should participate in the white man's scheme. Any comments?

The basis for that scene was Robeson's questioning whether a black man, oppressed by his country, should bear arms for it and against the Soviets. His position was later echoed by Muhammad Ali's famous Vietnam era protest, "No Vietnamese ever called me a nigger." Matters of race, of belonging, and with whom or with what we identify, and under what circumstances, and with what caveats are front and center in *All Man's Land*. For these patriots—I mean the buffalo soldiers—citizenship, recognition, and loyalty came with compromise and sacrifice for the Christian white man's mission—manifest destiny.

You use the n-word unabashedly in the text. Any comment regarding the offense it could cause?

Its use is realistic. Benjamin's fight is against racism. Those who use it get what's coming to them.

What would you say to critics who might suggest that *All Man's Land* appropriates a great man's legacy?

I didn't write it for them. I wrote it for him. The young man behind this novel wrote it with nothing short of reverence for Paul Robeson. Sadly, Robeson is only great to those who know him, and they are now shockingly few. It's troubling that three decades on, he has faded even further from public consciousness.

Why might this be?

Perhaps because [air quotes] "It's Complicated" with Paul Robeson. To try to explain him—which is a form of excusing him—gets you stuck in a quagmire. Nevertheless, the absence of this giant of the 20th century from *The Undefeated*'s list of "African Americans Who Shook Up the World" should leave us asking why. Was it his politics? Was it some of the songs he sang, some of the films he appeared in? Or was he simply overlooked? Nobody else shook up the world in quite the way Paul Robeson did. But his complicated story is best left to his biographers.

And yet you think this—a novel—could help bring the public closer to Robeson.

Something should. When [the movie] *12 Years a Slave* came out, its director announced his intention to shoot a Paul Robeson biopic next. Well, six years later, where is it? Its nonexistence speaks volumes.

But what would you say to the reader who questions why their introduction to him should come in the form of what could fairly be called a highly fictionalized tribute, rather than from a straightforward biography?

Paul Robeson should make his first impression through his music, that great voice and soul. But if *All Man's Land* is a person's point of discovery of this monumental American, then exploration of his music and life should follow. That was my hope for the book in 1990 when I completed the first draft, and it remains so today.